Justice at Buffalo Gap

Sanford Bates

ISBN:1547242310
ISBN-13:9781547242313

To Ron and Mary Bates.

Chapter 1

The rider tugged the brim of his hat down upon his brow shading his eyes from the glare of the dropping sun. Traveling west most of the day had kept the sun's rays upon the man's face. The rider and his horse had been making their way across the grasslands of the southern part of the Dakota Territory in the direction of the Black Hills.

The horse under the rider was medium sized and plain in appearance with no distinguishing marks upon its chestnut hide. Though not large, the animal was well proportioned and, even from a distance, one could tell it was bred for stamina more than for speed. The horse's gait was leisurely revealing that the rider and horse were in no great hurry to reach their destination.

The man upon the horse was of medium height with a long body and strong shoulders. His hair was dark, like the space in between stars in the night sky and it came down just below his ears. His skin was ruddy and it was easy to see if it was exposed to the sun for an extended period of time it would burn. Even so, his face was strong and confident and sported two days' growth of stubble. His dress consisted of a striped shirt, denim pants, sack coat, and the hat upon his head was a well-used tan Stetson. The jeans and sack coat both showed wear, one in the knees and the other in the elbows. Around his waist was strapped a light brown holster containing a single pistol that rode on his right hip. Along the right side of the horse was a scabbard that carried a well-used 1866 "Yellowboy" Winchester rifle.

The man's deep brown eyes were determined as he scanned the grassland around him. He rode straight in the saddle holding the reins lightly within his left hand and giving a tug once in a while to keep the horse headed west. The two had been traveling since right after sunup. This was their second day out from Pine Ridge, and their destination was Buffalo Gap, which the rider hoped to reach before dark. The trip had been uneventful so far. They had met no one along the way, which was a bit surprising to the man in the saddle since this was Lakota Indian country. He had expected to see them, even if he didn't come in direct contact. But up to this point, he had not seen any human, Indian or white.

The rider knew it didn't necessarily mean they weren't around. The Lakota in this area were known for choosing when and where they made contact with those outside their clan. Even though trees were few and far between, they would not show themselves until you were right upon them. This is why the rider surveyed the ground from left to right and right to left continually. He didn't fear the Lakota but he didn't want to be caught off guard if they were about.

The sea of grass all about the man and his horse had dominated the scenery since leaving Pine Ridge the day before. There had been trees along the streams that had crisscrossed their path, but for most of the way, the land was flat with some rolling hills covered mainly with grass. Looking ahead the rider saw that this was about to change. Again, he was coming upon another stream and this one was fairly large. The view in front of him was a solid line of cottonwoods. He perceived the stream had some width to it by how dense the cottonwoods were as they led to the edge of the stream. His horse's head lifted and its gate quickened as he heard the sound of flowing water.

The trees and under growth were thick along the stream though there were open patches intermittently along the edge of the stream. The pair found their way to the stream's bank through one of these openings. The chestnut horse quickly dipped his nose into the water. The rider quietly sat in the saddle and cautiously inspected the stream from right to left. Seeing nothing unusual, he was about to swing down out of the saddle to get his own drink, when he caught a faint noise to his right. It was brief and so slight that after a moment's silence he figured his ears were playing tricks. Then the sound came again, muffled, but from the same direction. It continued for several seconds and this time there was no doubt of his hearing. There definitely was something off to his right farther up the streambed and in amongst the cottonwoods. Curious, the rider gently pulled on the reins leading his horse away from the river in the direction they had come. Twenty yards or so back from the river the cottonwoods thinned out enough that the rider was able to turn left into the trees and head in the direction of the sound. There was still some undergrowth, but not enough to prevent the horse from navigating with ease around the trees. The man gently guided the horse, stopping every few yards to listen. The noise wasn't continuous, but occurred often enough that he and the horse were able to continue in the direction of the sound. After covering some forty yards and stopping and starting several times to listen, the two came to an open area in the cottonwoods. The rider brought his horse to a stop at the edge of the clearing and inspected it from within the trees. The area was approximately thirty yards across. The length was over twice as long with both ends narrowing to six-foot wide paths which wound through the trees, one to the right reaching east toward the open grassland and the one to the left leading down to the stream's edge.

Across the clearing just to his left, the rider observed the source of the noise. There were three men, one an Indian, the other two white men. The Indian was in a bad way. He was strapped with his back against one of the cottonwoods with his arms pulled back around each side and his hands, it would seem, tied together. This drew his back against the tree so tight movement was close to impossible.

The Indian's upper body was bare exposing a dark skinned and wiry body with a small frame. From his waist down he was adorned with elk hide pants and on his feet were colorful beaded moccasins. The dark black wispy hair on his head was parted in the middle and came down to his chest on each side of his face. The ends were tied off with red strips of cloth. His eyes were dark and fierce, looking straight ahead. Determination on his face.

Several injuries could be seen upon his chest and torso, injuries that were quite recent. They were not lacerations or cuts. Peering through the branches of the cottonwoods the rider guessed them to be burns. His attention turned to the other two men. Both their backs were to the rider. The one to the left turned in the direction of a small campfire delivering a generous flame with no smoke. The man reached for something sticking out of the fire and grasped it with his right hand. The end glowed a bright orange and yellow. Some sort of iron rod, thought the rider.

The rider scrutinized the face of the man holding the iron rod; it was long with a bulbous nose that dominated the entire face. A patchy red beard that needed grooming sprouted from his cheeks and chin. His smile revealed the wickedness the rider was soon to observe from these two. The red bearded man's partner was plump and short with a large head covered with light brown hair that was as unkempt as his friend's beard. As the man with the iron rod stepped toward the Indian the plump man spoke, " Been long enough, give him anudder taste of the fire Sid."

"Don't you worry none," answered Sid as he stepped toward the Indian, "I'm fixing to show this Lakota savage we'z in charge of this country."

Sid lowered the glowing end of the iron rod near the Lakota's chest just below the left pectoral muscle stopping less than an inch above the Indian's skin. The Lakota Indian kept his eyes straight ahead and his mouth rigid. He knew what was coming but showed no signs of weakness or fear.

"So, savage," snarled Sid, "you's think you's tough? This hot poker says differnt!"

Sid then laid the glowing end of the rod onto the skin of the Indian. The Indian grimaced and his body pulled to the left in reaction to the heat and pain, but he made no sound.

Sid's partner laughed heartily then said, "Yohwee. "Looka em squirm!"

The rider in the trees took this all in and was appalled at seeing the two treating the Indian in such a way. He contemplated his next move. Should he intervene or should he move on? None of the three knew he was there, he could easily ride away and no one would be the wiser. Besides, it seemed every time he got involved in other people's business, it always brought grief his way. That's how it had happened in New York City a year and a half ago, and then again in Tulsa, Oklahoma six months ago. He had done what he thought was right and ended up being entwined in political and family issues. Fortunately, each time he was able to weather the storm and free himself from the corruption of the incidents.

On the other hand, this definitely was another situation that was not right. What these two were doing to the Lakota was against human decency. It mattered not that the one being tortured was an Indian. His instinct encouraged him to leave it alone and to resume his travels to Buffalo Gap, but his conscience demanded that he do something to stop the brutality in the clearing.

The man called Sid was placing the iron rod back in the fire when the rider commanded the chestnut to enter the clearing. At first the two men did not notice the rider and his horse when they came out from the shade of the cottonwoods, their eyes were focused on the iron rod in the fire. The rider casually guided his horse in the direction of the three men scanning the area without taking his eyes off the two white men. He rapidly observed two horses with saddles, a mule packed with mining equipment (shovels, pickaxes and pans) and items for camp living, ropes, rolled blankets, canvas and poles. These animals were tied to two of the cottonwoods some fifteen yards on the other side of the fire.

The rider continued his approached without detection until his horse walked across an area that had numerous large stones. The sound of hoofs on stone caught the attention of the two white men and the Lakota warrior. Sid and his partner froze for a second surprised to see another person within the clearing. They both recovered quickly with Sid reaching for the pistol tucked in his belt. Drawing it, he said, "Whow there mister, no need to come closer."

The rider lightly pulled on the reins and the chestnut stopped. He surveyed the two miners taking in all that was before him. The pistol Sid was holding looked to be a Colt Navy type very old and very worn. The other miner had pulled a similar looking pistol from a holster on his right hip. The way the two miners held the pistols revealed they were not experts in gun handling, though their demeanor showed they would not be afraid to use them.

The rider broke the silence and calmly said, "Take it easy. No need to get defensive."

Sid growled back, "Defensive ha! We just don't like you's sneaken up on us."

The rider shifted in the saddle and said, "Sorry you see it that way. That's not my intention, I was just passing through and came upon you unexpectedly." The rider slowly reached up to his hat and pushed it slightly up his forehead then added, "Though I am a bit curious."

"Yah, what about!" snapped Sid's partner.

"Well, I'm curious as to why you're treating this man the way you are?" returned the rider nodding his head in the direction of the Lakota Indian.

Sid responded, "Don't see it's any of your business."

"Oh, but I disagree." said the rider as he slowly pulled his feet out of the stirrups of his saddle.

"Your actions would never be accepted in civilized society, and I'm a part of the civilized society of this country.

" These savages ain't from our society, they not civilized, they butcher our folk without reason." shot back Sid waving his pistol toward the Lakota.

"That's right stranger. We is doing our folk a favor by teaching this Indian not to mess with our own." added Sid's partner.

The two miners shifted uneasily where they stood when the rider remained silent. They kept their eyes along with their pistols upon the rider not sure of what his next move might be. The rider then spoke, " Did this Lakota treat you poorly?"

Sid and his partner looked at each other then back to the rider.

"Not exactly," responded Sid, "but he will, just like the rest of em. It's just a matter a time."

"It sounds to me as if you're placing blame," said the rider, somewhat accusingly, then added, "it doesn't really matter what your reasons are, nothing will make what you are doing right."

Raising his pistol so that it pointed directly at the rider, Sid's partner said deliberately, "We don't care much what's yous think. This is our business, not yours, so move on!"

"Can't do that," returned the rider waving the hand holding the reins unhurriedly toward the Indian. At the same time he lowered his right hand close to his own pistol. Unaware of the rider's movement the two minors kept their eyes on the eyes of the man on the horse.

The rider continued, "What you are doing is wrong and it stops now! You have a choice. You can untie the Indian and we all go our separate way, or this gets nasty."

Sid's eyebrows raised puzzled and he said, "What makes yous think you can do something to stop us? Weez both got you covered."

"Well, you two..." the rider suddenly let himself slide down the side of his horse grabbing onto the horse's mane with his left hand while at the same time pulling his pistol from his holster. As he was sliding down the side of his horse the rider heard two shots fired. Both shots must have passed over his horse for the animal didn't act as though either bullet had hit it. Once on the ground, the rider quickly took a look in the direction of the two miners under the jaw of the chestnut. Sid was crouched where he had been standing peering furtively in the direction of the horse. Sid's partner was stumbling toward the miners' horses. The rider brought his gun up and let off two quick shots. The first bullet tore into the miner's shoulder twisting him to his right, the second bullet found the middle of his chest dropping the man to the ground like a sack of wheat from a wagon.

The rider looked for Sid's partner. He was still traversing toward the horses but as he did so he took a couple of reckless shots in the direction of the rider and his horse. Both bullets kicked up dirt just to the right of the rider. The man from Pine Ridge raised his pistol and sighted down his barrel putting the miner directly in his sights then pulled the trigger. The handgun kicked backwards and the miner slumped to the ground with a grunt. The rider remained crouched behind his horse waiting to see if there was a response from the downed miner. The miner just lay where he had fallen moaning softly. After a short while the rider, sensing there was no threat from the wounded man, gingerly made his way toward the miner with pistol ready.

The man was on his side holding his hand over the wound. When the rider came within fifteen yards the miner propped himself up on his shoulder. With a small cry of pain, he turned his head to face the man that had shot him. The miner's breathing had become labored. The rider surmised the bullet had entered the man's lung.

"You's fast, you's and the gun," scowled the miner.

"Sorry it had to turn out this way," replied the rider shaking his head.

"I gave you an opportunity to end this peacefully and you and your partner chose otherwise."

"Maybe so," returned the miner wincing, "but weez was taken care of our own and you's allowed the savages to carry on against our people."

"I'm still not convinced your actions against this man were right," insisted the rider.

"That's the problem he's no man, less than human, deserved what he got," spat the miner. "Anyway, I'm done for, it don't matter for me none now."

Reaching for his pistol next to him he added, "You's got to pay."

"Don't do---" is all the rider could get out before the miner had the pistol and was lifting it towards him. Just as the barrel of the miner's gun was lining up on the rider the rider fired his own pistol twice in quick succession. The miner fell back as the two bullets slammed into his chest. He lay there still as rock. Taking a few steps toward the downed man the rider examined the body closely. The plump miner remained motionless.

The rider found the man's pistol on the ground quickly, picked it up and threw it toward the fire. He then turned back to the man on the ground and rolled him onto his back. He was dead. Two holes in the chest with an expressionless face was evidence enough this man no longer was with the living.

The rider then crossed over to where Sid was lying and confirmed that he was dead also. Looking in the direction of the Lakota at the tree the Indian showed no emotion as he looked back at the rider. The rider walked over and stood in front of the Indian.

"You speak English? "asked the rider.

The Lakota shook his head.

"Ok. We'll have to do it the hard way, "said the rider.

With that he gestured with his hands that he was going to cut the Indian free. From his pants, he dug out a folding knife. Opening one of the blades he moved to the other side of the tree. Once the rope had been cut the Lakota pulled off what remained around his wrists and then walked to the miner's horses and mule. Digging through the materials packed on the back of the mule the Lakota pulled a Sharps Rifle from beneath the pick axes and shovels. Moving to the horses he removed a leather pouch hanging from the saddle horn of the nearest horse. This he placed over his head and around his neck letting the pouch hang on his hip.

The rider took this all in while waiting next to the tree. After placing the pouch on his body the Lakota returned to where the rider was standing and through hand movements thanked him. The rider waving his hand showed thanks was not necessary. He then pointed to himself and said, "My name is Brian," continuing to tap his chest he repeated his name two more times. On the second time the Lakota held up his hand and nodded his head slowly.

He spoke for the first time, "Kohanna," as he lightly tapped his own chest.

"Good," said Brian nodding his head in response. Pointing at the Lakota Brian spoke his name, "Kohanna?"

The Lakota nodded again then pointed at the rider and said, "Brian." Brian looking at the wounds on the Lakota's motioned if Kohanna was all right. The Lakota nodded that he was. Brian then tried asking what had happened, how he gotten himself in the predicament with the miners. This was not so easy. So many actions and abstract concepts it was difficult to get across what he wanted to know. He finally resorted to drawing pictures in the dirt along with hand gestures to get his question understood. Through similar methods the Lakota was able to give Brian a brief description what had occurred.

Kohanna had been riding through the clearing to the stream when his horse happened upon a rattlesnake. Startled, the horse reared and threw Kohanna. As he was dropping to the ground the back of his head slammed on a limb of a cottonwood knocking him unconscious. When he came to, he was tied to the tree and the miners were building the fire.

This answered the how and why the Lakota came to be in the clearing tied to a tree and being brutally treated. The next question was, what next? Kohanna let it be known that he was fine to travel on his own and they both decided Kohanna could take one of the horses since his horse had taken off. They stripped the saddle off the nearest horse and Kohanna with rifle in hand hopped up on the bare back. The horse shied at first but settled down quickly under the skilled Lakota rider's hand.

Brian had indicated that he needed to stay and prepare to take the two miners, the horse, mule and gear into Buffalo Gap. Kohanna looked into the eyes of Brian, then leaned down toward him with an outstretched hand. Brian reached up to take the hand of the Lakota but the Indian grasped the inside of his forearm and squeezed hard. Kohanna never took his eyes off those of Brian's as they grasped each other's arms. Brian understood the Lakota was deeply grateful for rescuing him. Then Kohanna let go, straightened onto the back of the horse pulled on the reins and guided the horse toward the east through the cottonwoods into the prairie beyond. Brian watched him until he disappeared down the trail then turned and began the business of getting the miners and their gear ready to take to Buffalo Gap.

Chapter 2

The sun dipping close to the horizon showed there was just over an hour of daylight left as Brian and his group of horses and mule approached the outskirts of Buffalo Gap. Brian could see already from a distance that the town was small having one street that stretched maybe two or three blocks. The buildings were relatively new, the town coming into existence just recently because of the gold discovered in the Black Hills to the north. Brian surmised the town would not remain small for long with the potential of gold drawing many gold seekers to the area. Buffalo Gap would be a nice jumping off place for many that came through this part of the country heading to the gold fields.

As he got closer, Brian noticed there were a few outlying buildings. These looked to be homes and a few storage buildings. Looking down the street Brian saw numerous people wandering up and down the street or crossing from one side to the other. Coming to the first building, he recognized it to be the town's stable and blacksmith. He would need to return with the miner's horse and mule when he had finished his business with the sheriff. Right now, he wanted to get to the sheriff's office and explain the two dead bodies he had with him. As he rode up the street all eyes were upon him and his convoy. Brian figured he presented quite a sight leading a horse and mule with a dead body slumped over each. He kept his eyes forward, not acknowledging the stares that were following him as he moved up the middle of the street.

Continuing on his way into town, he spotted the office of the sheriff to his left about halfway up the block. Even though he was itching to get to the sheriff he suppressed the urge to increase his speed and calmly guided his horse toward the office. The town folk continued to stop and look in his direction with some even pointing as they murmured to each other. Most were rough looking men, most likely miners or miners to be. There were a few women about, but not the type that would be wives of respectable men. But this was not surprising. It wasn't a town expecting families to move into the area.

As Brian came up before the building with the word sheriff in large bold letters above its door, the door opened and a tall man with keen eyes stepped out of the office. On the left side of the clean well-pressed vest he wore was a star, the sheriff. As the sheriff moved away from the door a second man came through. This second man was almost as tall as the sheriff and Brian couldn't miss the dark thick bushy mustache he sported. His face was hard and showed signs of being in the sun, the skin was dark and wrinkled.

After inspecting Brian and his animals, the sheriff said with a curious tone, " It would seem you have some explaining to do."

"It would seem so," agreed Brian.

"It looks to be Sid and his buddy Jed," said the man with the mustache while stepping into the street.

"Not surprising," offered the sheriff with contempt in his voice. Then looking back to Brian, he asked, "What's the story?"

"Well sir, I was on my way to Buffalo Gap from Pine Ridge when I came across these two about five miles south of here. They had a Lakota Warrior tied to a tree and were torturing him with a hot iron rod. In no uncertain terms, I told them to stop and they responded by taking shots at me with their pistols. I defended myself and the two ended up as you see them," responded Brian tilting his head toward the two dead bodies.

"Is that right?" said the sheriff folding his arms across his chest, then asked "how do we know what you say is the truth? What proof do you have?"

Brian took his hat off and ran his fingers through his hair. After placing it back on his head he answered, "As I stand before you here on this street I have no definite proof. If we could speak to the Lakota Warrior he could collaborate my story but my guess is that his words wouldn't carry much weight in this town."

"True, the Indian, for most people in town wouldn't make much of an alibi," agreed the sheriff.

"Sheriff, I'm not looking for trouble. Looking at it now, I just happened to be in the wrong place at the wrong time," insisted Brian.

"Yes it would seem you have brought some unwanted difficulty your way," said the sheriff.

The man with the mustache interrupted speaking to the sheriff, "Luke these two on the horse and mule have both been shot from the front. What he says could be true."

"That definitely helps," responded the sheriff taking two steps to his right to get a better look at the two dead men. "The other thing in your favor mister are these two," pointing toward the two dead men, "They have been a nasty nuisance to the town and surrounding area since arriving a couple of months ago."

"Yah," piped the man with the mustache, "this isn't the first time these two have been mixed up in something like this. Just last week---"

"Never mind that now," cut in the sheriff, "what needs to be done at the moment is get these two dead bodies taken care of."

The sheriff pulled a pocket watch from the pocket of his vest checked the time then said, "Jasper it's a bit late, but take these two bodies over to Doc McMillan and have him take care of them."

"Sure thing sheriff," said Jasper grabbing the reins of the horse and the mule's rope and heading north up the street.

Motioning to Brian, the sheriff commanded, "Let's go into my office and we'll continue our chat about what happened to Sid and Jed."

Brian threw his right leg over the back of the saddle and lowered himself to the ground. Wrapping the reins around the railing in front of the sheriff's office he made sure the horse was secure then followed the lawman into his office. Passing through the door Brian found himself in a jail that looked comparable to jails he had visited before. This one had ample office space that contained a small desk off to the right next to the wall. On the desk, Brian noticed a kerosene lamp, two neatly stacked piles of paper, and a pen with an inkwell. Up behind the desk lying across two pegs on the wall was a coach shotgun. At the back of the room was a single cell that was fronted by iron bars that contained a solitary door. The rest of the cell was comprised of brick with a bed along the left wall.

The sheriff pointed to a plain wooden chair in front of the small desk offering Brian a place to sit down, while he himself maneuvered around the desk and took the seat behind it. When they were both seated the sheriff placed his forearms on top of the desk and clasped his hands together then locked his eyes on Brian's face and said, "We haven't been properly introduced, my name is Luke Baker the sheriff of Buffalo Gap."

"Brian Dolan," said Brian leaning toward the desk and offering his hand. The sheriff took it and they shook firmly. After Brian sat back in his chair the sheriff asked, "What about this Indian you helped? What can you tell me about him? "

"Not much," replied Brian rubbing his chin with his right hand. "The only thing for sure I can give you is his name, Kohanna."

"Ah yes, I know of him," said the sheriff nodding his head, then added, "Seems to be some sort of leader of the Lakota in the area. I don't know for sure if he is their chief but the Indians around here follow his lead."

"I couldn't enlighten you on that, the man doesn't speak English and our conversation was limited to hand signals and picture drawing in the dirt," said Brian in return.

"Yes I can understand that," acknowledged the sheriff getting up from the desk walking over to the wall to his left. Studying the pictures on the wall he continued, "He hasn't been a problem, in fact he appears to have kept the Indian population pretty friendly with the white folk in these parts. As I mentioned earlier, I don't think there will be much fuss about these two. Sid and Jed had already shown they were not the kind of men we like to welcome to Buffalo Gap.

Turning to face Brian he asked inquisitively, " What about you, what brings you to these parts?"

Shifting his body so that he faced the sheriff Brian replied, "I'm here on business."

"And what business would that be?"

"It has to do with Virgil Langston."

The sheriff sat down on the corner of his desk folded his arms across his chest and said, "Do you know Mr. Langston?"

"Yes I do," answered Brian, "We worked together when I was in New York a couple years back."

"If I'm not intruding, what business do you have with Mr. Langston?"

"I'll tell you this much. He sent me a letter thinking I was still in New York and it finally caught up with me when I was in Topeka Kansas. His proposal in the letter piqued my interest and that's why I am here. But until I get a chance to see Virgil personally I prefer not to discuss it further."

"Fair enough," said the sheriff with no animosity.

Getting up from the desk the sheriff sauntered over to the window at

the front of the room pulled back the curtain and looked out into the street. Without taking his gaze from the street he asked, "Did Mr. Langston let you know his position in this town?"
"Not exactly," responded Brian getting up from his chair and facing the sheriff. "He did mention his involvement with the gold mining going on in the Black Hills region."

The sheriff let the curtain fall back over the window and rotated his head in the direction of Brian and said with a touch of regret in his voice, "Yes he is involved for sure. You could say he pretty much controls all of what goes on when it comes to mining in these parts."

Just then the door to the office opened and through the doorway entered a small man with a slight frame and receded hairline. His face matched his body, it was thin with spectacles sitting on a pointed nose. He wore an apron of sorts that reached from his chest down to his ankles.

"Sheriff Baker I just saw Jasper with those two unruly miners heading up the street, and it looked as though they were dead!" blurted the thin man slamming the door shut behind him.

"Take it easy Hans," commanded the sheriff calmly.

"But, what happened!" shot Hans with excitement.

"There was a little incident just south of town and Sid and Jasper came out on the short end of it. All has been taken care of. There is no need for you to worry or for that matter anything to concern yourself with, "replied the sheriff.

Hans then noticed Brian standing next to the sheriff's desk and sheepishly looked from the sheriff to Brian then back to the sheriff.

"Sorry sheriff, I didn't realize you had a visitor," said Hans.

"Quite alright Hans, this is Brian Dolan. He's just arrived in town, " said the sheriff then looking at Brian he continued, "Brian this is Hans Friedman he runs the general store here in Buffalo Gap.

"Hello sir," said Hans to Brian.

"Pleased to meet you, "said Brian in return.

Turning his attention back to the sheriff Hans asked, "What about---"

The sheriff cut in, "Now Hans, I said everything is taken care of for the moment. You need not concern yourself right now, you'll find out soon enough the whole story but for now we are still conducting our investigation."

"I was just thinking, maybe it was Indians," said Hans with a worrisome tone.

"Indians did not kill those two," assured the sheriff moving to the door and opening it, "Now off you go, you have plenty to do at the store,"

"Okay sheriff, if you say so," said Hans striding to the door.

After Hans passed through the doorway sheriff Baker said to Brian, "I think this is a good time to go see Mr. Langston. His place of business is just up the street and I would be glad to show you the way."

"Sounds good," replied Brian.

Sheriff Baker waved for Brian to take the lead out of the office and Brian complied without hesitation. Once outside Brian waited as the sheriff locked the door and then they both stepped into the street.

"How about my horse sheriff, I would really like to get him settled for the night," said Brian.

"Don't worry about that. I'll have my deputy take your horse down to the stable after he's finished at Docs place." offered the sheriff nudging Brian's shoulder directing him up the street. " We'll be passing his establishment on the way."

"Thanks, much appreciated," said Brian responding to the nudge and walking along with the sheriff.

The two made their way up the street with the sheriff steering them across to the other side once they reached the doctors place of business. It was situated between the bank and what served as the hotel for the town. There were two men outside the entrance to the hotel as sheriff Baker and Dolan walked up to the doctor's office. They were deep in conversation and didn't notice the sheriff and Brian as they stepped up onto the wooden sidewalk that ran the length of the block. The sheriff had Brian remain outside while he went in and talked with the doctor and his deputy.

While the sheriff was inside Brian took the opportunity to study the town more thoroughly. He was immediately impressed with the modernization of the town. A town this size, this new, and with the clientele it garnered would usually just have what was necessary to make it operate. But Buffalo Gap had wooden sidewalks on both sides of the street, and it look as though there were a number of lampposts with kerosene lamps. Along with the stable he'd seen when he first entered the town, Brian now observed a general store, two saloons, a restaurant, and next to the restaurant was a building whose sign read Buffalo Mining Co.

The sheriff came out of the doctor's office and told Brian that all was taken care of, both the miners and giving the message about his horse to his deputy. He then directed Brian toward the Buffalo Mining Co. building just across the street. The two walked in silence until they reached the other side and Sheriff Baker said, "This is where you'll find Mr. Langston most of the time, even at this late hour in the day. He never knows when to call it a day when it comes to the mining business. Of course you may already know that from your time with him back in New York."

"Sounds like the same man," said Brian examining the building before him. Thoughts raced through his head as he thought back to his time in New York working with the man he was about to see again after two years. They had worked together closely back then and Brian had learned a lot about making money and all that goes with it. It was a good time for a while, but as with most things, it didn't last. Virgil Langston had taken on more than the business could handle and the two of them were unable to keep up with the needs of those they were doing business with. Their early success became their worst enemy and it all came crashing down upon them. In the end, they both ended up worse off than when they started, causing them to go in different directions. That was two years ago. Now he stood within thirty feet of making the man's acquaintance again.

Sheriff Baker led the way to the door of the Buffalo Mining Company, hesitated for a moment and then stepped inside followed by Brian. When the two men were inside Brian noticed right away this was an office inhabited by one who liked nice things and had the money to buy them. It wasn't a large office, but it was furnished elegantly. Directly in front of Sheriff Baker and Brian was an ornate table with two wooden chairs in front of it. Behind the table and along the back wall was a fine dark oak roll top desk that was neatly organized with numerous papers and envelopes stuffed in the shelves above the desktop. Sitting in between the table and the desk was a luxurious rolling office chair. Next to the desk on the right was a door leading to another room. Just like the sheriff's office, kerosene lamps illuminated the area with two burning brightly, one on the roll top desk, and the other on a file cabinet up against the left wall.

Seeing no one in the office, Sheriff Baker walked over to the table and gave the bell on it a quick ring. Shortly, the door at the back of the room opened and a well-dressed gentleman wearing a frock coat, low cut vest and a tied cravat entered the room. His hair matched his clothing, being combed neatly down tight to his scalp. His closely trimmed beard and mustache reflected his concern to detail. Seeing the two men in the office the sharply dressed gentleman looked back into the room he had just come through and announced, " Mr. Langston, Sheriff Baker is here with another gentleman."

From within the room came a deep voice, "Be right there."

Turning back to the Sheriff and Brian the man next to the door said, " Good to see you Sheriff, and who is this with you?" directing his attention to Brian.

"Jim," nodded Sheriff Baker, "This here is Brian Dolan, just arrived in town."

Just then the man from within the other room with the deep voice came through the door. He looked at the Sheriff then to Brian.

Then all of a sudden he shouted, "Sheriff, arrest this man!"

Chapter 3

Approaching nightfall further slowed the progress of a small detachment of Calvary traveling south from Fort Meade to Buffalo Gap. They had been moving at a crawl all day, and now would not reach the town until the next morning. Lieutenant William Carlson at the front of the column pulled on his horse's reins and peeled off to the left, moving to the back of the short line of horses and men. From the back of the column the lieutenant examined the detachment he was leading to Buffalo Gap. At the head was Sergeant Matt Halsey, a dedicated soldier who didn't necessarily follow the book when it came to army regulations. A good man to have in Indian Territory, he had shown his ability to adapt to the unorthodox methods of the Lakota and their allies during battle.

Next in line were two privates. One had been at fort Meade for over a year, the other was a green recruit assigned to the fort just a month ago. Following these two was the wagon that was to carry the shipment of gold from Buffalo Gap back to Fort Meade. Riding on the buckboard was Private Sam Henderson a lifer in the army who had been at the fort since it first came into existence. He was a rugged individual who never quite had his uniform in regulation form, but was an experienced fighter, especially on the prairies surrounding the Black Hills. Alongside Private Henderson and traveling with the army detail was the one person that was not connected to the fort through the government. Sarah Schuler ended up with Lieutenant Carlson and his detachment because she was passing through Fort Meade on her way to visit her uncle in Buffalo Gap. Reaching Fort Meade the day before this small party was to leave for Buffalo Gap was providence Sarah could not pass up. She was grateful for the guidance and protection that would get her to her destination in relative safety. It didn't take much effort to convince the commanding officer of Fort Meade to allow her to travel with the gold escorting detail since she indicated in no uncertain terms she would travel to Buffalo Gap on her own instead of waiting for the next civilian group heading that way.

Being a woman in such a group was odd but she wasn't vastly out of place in the clothing she wore. She had a light colored long sleeved cotton blouse tucked into a dark full-length brushed twill skirt. For footwear she wore laced up walking boots. The clothing fit comfortably over a slender five foot five-inch frame. She had an oval face, fair skin, a slender nose, and bright blue eyes. Her long wavy light auburn hair was partially covered by a plain sunhat with a blue ribbon that accentuated her eyes.

The final two soldiers bringing up the rear of the column were two more privates that had recently arrived at Fort Meade. This was their first duty away from the fort and Lieutenant Carlson hoped the rest of the trip would be uneventful. Having three young soldiers in their party was not what he desired if they ran into trouble. It would be nice for them to get some experience of the land, as well as with each other, before facing the kind of trouble this territory could give.

The lieutenant pulled a watch from his pants pocket to check the time and then looked west to the setting sun. Jamming the watch back in his pocket, he kneed his horse gently in the side and the horse responded with a gallop along the column back to the front. Once past Sergeant Halsey, he brought his horse to a stop in front of the line and raised his hand above his head. As the convoy came to a halt he said so all could hear, "The hour is late, we will set up camp for the night." Then to Sergeant Halsey he commanded, "Sergeant take care of the details."

"Yes Sir," replied the Sergeant. He then pulled on the reins guiding his horse to the right and back down the convoy barking orders to the soldiers as he went by. Each trooper broke from the column after the sergeant passed and attended to his duties. It took less than an hour to establish a secured encampment for the night. The horses were tethered together, the wagon taken off the trail, a campfire built, and two sentries placed on opposites sides of the camp. Private Henderson made sure the wagon was attended to so that their female companion had a comfortable place to sleep for the night. He laid two extra wool blankets on the floor of the wagon and created a tent like covering out of the canvas that was to cover the gold on the return trip.

As the men finished making camp, the sun had dropped below the horizon. Soon all were sitting around the central fire warming themselves in the coolness of the evening. Being mid-May, the nights on the prairie were still struggling to break from the cooler temperatures of the winter months. The coffee warming over the fire was a welcome drink to help wash down the day's dust and keep the traveler's hands warm. The soldiers sat around the fire on whatever they could find within close proximity of the camp, while Sarah was given a crate from the wagon that held various tools.

After taking a sip from his tin cup, Lieutenant Carlson, without moving his eyes from the fire asked, "Comfortable Miss Schuler?"

"Yes, quite comfortable," replied Sarah turning her head to look at the lieutenant. "I would like to thank you again for your hospitality since leaving Fort Meade."

"I'll be honest, Miss Schuler, at first I wasn't too keen on the idea," said Lieutenant Carlson, eyes still on the fire.

"I can understand that," said Sarah rubbing her hands slowly around the tin cup holding her coffee. "Just what you needed, a woman tagging along with you and your men," she added playfully.

"Exactly ma'am," agreed the Lieutenant. "But on the other hand, we work for the government and we are here to serve the people of this nation," added Carlson with no animosity.

"Well, still, I appreciate it," offered Sarah warmly.

"Your most welcome," said Carlson.

From the other side of the fire Sergeant Halsey spoke, "Miss Schuler, if I may ask, what brings you out to these parts in the first place?"

"I am heading to Buffalo Gap to visit my uncle," answered Sarah.

"Your uncle eh," grunted the Sergeant.

"Yes, my mother received an invitation to come out west and visit her brother in-law but she is too ill to make the trip," related Sarah.

"I'm sorry about your mother ma'am," interjected Lieutenant Carlson.

"Thank you, Lieutenant for your concern," replied Sarah, "but, she is comfortable and being well taken care of by her sister."

"So you came in place of your mother?" asked Sergeant Halsey.

"That's right. As mother wasn't well enough to travel, we agreed that I should make the trip for her. Even though my uncle wasn't specific about why he wanted her to visit, his excitement was quite evident in the letter," replied Sarah.

"Who is your uncle?" inquired one of the privates sitting to the Sergeant's right.

" His name is Virgil Langston," she answered.

There was a shrill whistle from Sergeant Halsey and then he said, "Langston, he's quite the big man in these parts."

" Is that right, how so?" asked Sarah

"He pretty much controls the mining that goes on in and around Buffalo Gap. He's the one that has put Buffalo Gap on the map, so to speak," answered Halsey.

"I had no idea," said Sarah with raised eyebrows, "the last we had heard of uncle Virgil was when he was in New Orleans working for some riverboat outfit. That was over a year ago."

"Well it would seem your uncle has made his way north and changed his vocation," said the private to Halsey's right as he tossed what coffee remained in his cup into the fire.

"Yes it would," agreed Sarah pulling her riding coat down over her shoulders, "and according to you Sergeant it would also seem his fortune has changed for the better."

There was silence then as everyone around the fire looked straight into the flames of the fire contemplating their own thoughts. Then the Lieutenant broke the silence and spoke to Sarah.

"Somebody was going to profit from the gold in and around the Black Hills. It turns out your uncle is one of them."

Sarah turned and spoke directly to Carlson. "I guess maybe that's the excitement we felt from his letter to us. If he has become successful, as Sergeant Halsey says, then I understand why he wanted my mother to come visit."

"If I'm not being too nosy, why would your uncle's success cause him to invite your mother, an Easterner I presume, to come out here in the middle of nowhere far from civilization?" asked the private.

Sarah turned back to the fire, leaned over her lap and grabbed the end of one of the branches smoldering in the campfire and stabbed at the coals causing the dying flame to expand.

"That's quite all right," said Sarah tossing the branch gently onto the fire, " you're not being nosy, but, I will try to make a long story as short as possible. My uncle married my mother's sister without the blessing of most of my family. Uncle Virgil was kind of a drifter who came into my aunt's life and swept her off her feet so to speak. He treated her well and all but he didn't have a steady way to support the two of them. So when they got married most of the family considered him a slacker and didn't give their blessing. After a short time he went to New York City to pursue an opportunity that offered quick money. He left my aunt behind until he had settled in and earned enough for her to join him. Well, she became ill shortly after his departure and word was sent he should return. He didn't return right away. He had been on the verge of becoming very prosperous, so he remained in New York. My aunt's health worsened, and by the time my uncle did return, it was too late." Sarah paused, looking into the tin cup she was holding, then continued. "Except for my mother, the family wouldn't forgive him. He hasn't been welcomed since the funeral. I think my uncle wants make up for what happened earlier. But that is only a guess on my part."

"That's quite a story!" exclaimed the private.

"How is it your mother could forgive this guy?" interjected Halsey somewhat disgusted.

"She's a Christian. The bible tells us to forgive," replied Sarah.

"Your mother is a believer?" asked the Lieutenant.

"Yes she is," replied Sarah.

"And you?" questioned the Lieutenant.

"Yes, I am also," said Sarah without hesitation.

Just then the private on guard called out to Sergeant Halsey. All heads turned in the direction of the voice as Sergeant Halsey jumped to his feet and walked briskly to where the private had called. Those that remained around the fire could see the outlines of the two men as they talked but couldn't make out the words they were saying as the two soldiers talked in whispers.

After a minute the sergeant motioned for the lieutenant to come over to them. The lieutenant calmly got to his feet and walked to where the two men were and a brief conversation between the sergeant and the lieutenant commenced. At the end of their conversation, the lieutenant came back to the campfire and said, "There is a possibility we have company somewhere out on the prairie," then, turning in the direction of Sarah, the lieutenant calmly continued. "There is no reason to be alarmed, Miss Schuler. Private Biggs heard some rustling some twenty yards beyond where he is standing. It could be anything, maybe just a curious coyote. But to be on the safe side, would you please move next to the wagon while we investigate."

Sarah nodded to the lieutenant and then stepped quickly over to the wagon where she placed her back against the front wheel and gazed in the direction of Private Biggs. Sergeant Halsey had by then commanded Private Dooley to go with Private Biggs and search the area where the noise had been heard. The Private quickly jumped to his feet and hurried over to the wagon where he snatched up his Sharps Carbine and joined Biggs. The two then moved out together cautiously, separating as they proceeded further into the darkness. After they had passed beyond the light of the campfire's flames, only their silhouettes were visible.

Those within the perimeter of the camp followed the outlines of the two privates as they moved slowly into the area Private Biggs had pointed out to the lieutenant. After several minutes of searching, the two expanded their investigation with Biggs going to the left and Dooley going to the right. The soldiers worked their way slowly in a circle around the camp. They were carefully probing the darkness trying to see or hear any intruder that might be lurking just beyond the light.

Sarah, too, peered into the darkness trying to see what lay out beyond the edge of the camp. She was surprised how calm she felt standing next to the wagon. Living on the east coast she had heard frightening tales of life in the west. She had thought she would be more anxious, but was surprised to feel a peace within herself that allowed her to be focused on the events taking place around her without real fear.

The two privates eventually worked their way around the camp until they came together on the opposite side. Nothing suggested that there was any immediate danger. Lieutenant Carlson returned to the middle of the camp followed by Sergeant Halsey. Standing next to the fire Lieutenant Carlson said, " Nothing seems to be prowling out in the darkness at the moment, but to be safe, I suggest that Miss Schuler turn in, and the rest of us will take turns on guard duty throughout the night. "

Lieutenant Carlson gave orders to his men to prepare the camp for the night, and to place two men on the first shift of sentry duty. While this was occurring, Sarah climbed into the wagon and prepared to sleep. She decided not to change the clothes she was wearing. Danger was present, and she would rather face the emergency fully dressed. Sarah took off her riding coat and crawled in between the two blankets feet first, she then pulled the top blanket up to her neck. While lying on her back she flung the riding coat on top of the blanket. She finished her preparations by sliding the satchel bag full of clothing under her head. All considered, she felt quite snug for the night. As she lay there staring up at the make shift tent above her head, she thanked God for bringing her through another day, and asked that he protect their little band throughout the night. She then closed her eyes and attempted to go to sleep. As it turned out, she wasn't able to drift off to sleep until well after midnight, thinking about what may or may not be creeping around out on the prairie.

Chapter 4

After shouting for Brian to be arrested, the man with the deep voice just stared intently at Brian with a look of distaste upon his face. Brian was so taken aback by this sudden accusation, that he found himself unable to make any response. He just stared back dumbfounded. Sheriff Baker broke the silence, "Mr. Langston, I don't quite understand?"

Just then the look of distaste upon Mr. Langston's face changed into a huge smile showing big white teeth.

"Gotcha!" exclaimed Langston laughing uproariously. He held out his right hand, and stepping forward said, "Glad to see you made it, Brian. I was beginning to lose hope that you were ever coming."

Langston then grasped Brian's right hand that was hanging at his side and gave it a vigorous shaking. Brian was still in a bit of shock and didn't offer any resistance to the hearty handshake that traveled all the way to his shoulder.

"What's the matter Brian? Nothing to say after two years?" asked Langston through the huge smile on his face.

"I...I'm not sure what to say," said Brian pulling his hand from the grip of Langston, "I'm a bit confused. First you demand that I be arrested then you follow that with smiles and warm greetings."

"I was just playing with ya," said Langston with a wink. "Worked pretty good eh?"

"Yeah, for sure," agreed Brian letting the tension that had seized him subside a little.

"Take a load off your feet," offered Langston motioning to the two wooden chairs in front of the table, "You too Luke."

Brian and Luke settled themselves into the two chairs and Langston directed Jim to go into the back room and retrieve a bottle of whiskey and some glasses. Jim disappeared through the door and Langston moved to the other side of the table turning the big office chair toward the two men across the table and sat down. Virgil Langston sat tall in the chair as he looked across the table at the two men on the other side. Being six foot two and just over two hundred pounds, Langston was a commanding presence.

Swiveling in his fancy chair toward the roll top desk, Langston opened the top drawer and pulled out a wooden box. Turning back to the table he lifted the top of the box toward the Sheriff and Brian and asked, "Cigar?"

Although they both shook their heads, Langston took a cigar for himself and returned the box to the drawer. After lighting the cigar and taking several quick puffs he sat back in his chair and studied the man across the table, the man he hadn't seen in two years. He could tell from Brian's posture that the man he'd known two years before in New York was still there, but he could also detect there was something different. He couldn't quite put his finger on what that difference was but there it was, no doubt about it. Langston's concern, for the moment, was whether or not the difference was for the better.

"What have you been doing these past two years?" questioned Langston.

"Oh, a little of this, a little of that, whatever came my way," replied Brian with a non-committal shrug.

"Is that so," said Langston blowing cigar smoke into the air above his head. "It must not have been that exciting or I wouldn't find you sitting across the table from me now."

At that moment Jim came into the room carrying a tray that held four small glasses and what looked like a full bottle of whiskey.

"Excellent!" barked Langston sitting up in his chair. “Jim, pour us each a glass and one for yourself."

Jim set the tray on top of the file cabinet and half-filled each glass with whiskey. He then handed a glass to each of the men sitting around the table. After Jim took the last glass from the tray Langston held up his glass and said with the broad smile still upon his face, "Drink up men. Now that Brian Dolan is here, I see the future of Buffalo Gap being brighter than ever." He downed the whole glass of whiskey and slammed the empty glass onto the table. Luke and Brian shared a perplexed glance. Luke then shrugged his shoulders and took a drink from his glass. Brian followed suit by downing half his glass and placing it back on the table.

" I can see from the look on your faces you are a bit confused," said Langston pulling his chair up to the table and placing his elbows on top and clasping his hands together. "Let me explain. For the past nine months, Buffalo Gap has grown from being a wide spot in the road to what you see today. Though not large, it is a town that has all the amenities needed to satisfy most people's needs. And all this is due, of course, to the gold that was discovered in the Black Hills just to the north of us. It looks as though the gold is not going to dry up any time soon. With our initial claims and investments in the area, we have been able to get ahead of the competition. Unfortunately, more and more people flowing into the region and wanting their piece of the pie has cut into our profits. That's where you come in Brian. As a team we could be bring the success of this operation to a new level."

"If you remember Virgil our time together in New York ended in a miserable failure," interjected Brian.

"Yes, yes I know, but I've learned a thing or two since that time and I am much wiser when it comes to people and finance," returned Langston waving his hand, "I plan to avoid the pitfalls that snared us last time."

"Okay, so what's my role in all this?" asked Brian.

"Your part will be somewhat similar to what you did back in New York. Buffalo Gap Mining Company has grown to the point that I don't have the time to run things here in town as well as at the mines. I want you to be my foreman in the camps to oversee all that is going on there. That will free me up to take care of business from this end."

Langston held up his hand, "I know, I know you're asking yourself why you, why not someone here in Buffalo Gap? I'll tell you why. I have already tried two men and they just weren't up to the task. I still ended up doing both jobs. With you I know the job will get done and done well. That is if you are still the same man I worked with two years ago."

Brian took his glass from the table, examined its contents, then slowly took a drink. He carefully placed the empty glass back on the table. Looking at Langston he said," The job sounds interesting and I believe I can do the job you want, though it remains to be seen if I am the same man you knew two years ago."

"Great!" exclaimed Langston. "We can go over the details tomorrow morning, for now though, I am sure you are probably hungry and tired from your journey. I have some pressing business that can't wait but I'll have Sheriff Baker take you over to the Lucky Lady for a meal and then set you up for the night at our modest rooming house here in town. And don't fret, everything is on me. Glad to have you back Brian," said Langston getting to his feet and stretching his hand out. Brian stood up shook Langston's hand. " Thanks for the job and for the rest, too," he said.

"I'll see you here at 9:30 tomorrow morning and well going over the particulars," said Langston.

"Tomorrow then," answered Brian.

Langston nodded to Sheriff Baker and then motioned to Jim to follow him into the back room leaving Brian and the sheriff alone once again in the office of the Buffalo Mining Company.

"Well I guess I'm to take you over to the Lucky Lady and get you some grub," said Sheriff Baker heading toward the door.

"I didn't realize how hungry I was until now," said Brian, "lead on."

The two men left the office and stepped out into the street with the sheriff heading back in the direction where the stables were located. By now, evening had come and in a short time the street lamps would be lit. As they walked up the street, Brian noticed the town was quiet except for the noise coming from just up the street to their right. He figured that's where they were heading for supper. Of all the places in town to harbor the most commotion the saloon would be the first choice. As the two progressed up the street the din coming from within the saloon grew louder.

When they reached the Lucky Lady, the sheriff paused at the doors and studied the room within. There was a bar that ran along the left wall of the establishment stretching almost the entire length. The rest of the room was outfitted for the patrons, with eight small tables and four chairs per table evenly spaced throughout the saloon. At the moment, six of the tables had their full complement of miners and cowboys. The other two tables had no one sitting at them. At the bar there were two more miners leaned up against the counter, each one nursing a drink.

Pushing on the swinging doors, Sheriff Baker said as he entered the saloon, "We're in luck, there are a couple of free tables. We won't have to wait too long to get our supper."

"Excellent!" responded Brian and he followed the sheriff into the saloon.

As they walked across the room, only three of the men at the tables turned their heads in the direction of the new comers. The rest were engrossed with their conversations. The farthest table from the doorway was in the middle of a card game with all four participants keenly watching the cards in their hands, as well as those on the table. Strolling to the nearest free table, Sheriff Baker sat down and gestured to the man behind the bar..

The man tending the bar had been watching the card game from behind the counter when he noticed the Sheriff signaling him from across the room. After wiping the counter top in front of him, he moved down to the far end of the bar, dropped the towel and walked nonchalantly toward the Sheriff and Brian.

"Jacob, how are things this evening?' inquired the sheriff.

"Busy as always," said Jacob tilting his head in the direction of the other tables, "so far it's been pretty calm."

"I think you have found the true gold mine in this area," said Sheriff Baker, "Your place seems to be pretty much full most every night and you don't have to be out in the weather or in the dirt and grime of the mine."

"That is true, but it does have its down side. If I was working a mine I wouldn't have to put up with unruly miners, cowboys or soldiers," said Jacob wiping his hands on the stained apron hanging from his waist. "It seems most evenings I have to deal with some sort of ruckus between the patrons."

"I suppose every job has its drawbacks," said Baker thoughtfully.

"What can I get you two?" asked Jacob, changing the subject.

"How about a couple of your famous steak dinners," replied Baker with a smile." Oh, and by the way, let me introduce my guest. This is Brian Dolan just arrived this evening. He's here to work for Langston out at the mines. "

Jacob studied Brian for a moment then said, "Welcome to Buffalo Gap and I wish you luck at the mines."

Brian was not sure how to take the latter part of his statement. He didn't know if the bar tender was wishing him luck at the new job or wishing him luck at what the mines might produce. Before he could question Jacob about his meaning, Jacob asked him directly, "How would you like your steak?"

"Medium is fine," answered Brian.

"Good, sheriff I know how you like yours. I'll get on em right away," said Jacob turning back to the bar.

The sheriff looked around the room examining each and every man. As he did so, he spoke to Brian without taking his eyes off the others in the saloon.

"Even though we are in the middle of nowhere the steak dinners here are quite good. Jacob has an experienced cook working for him. He came here three months ago to make his fortune digging for gold and found out it wasn't worth the time or effort. It was easy for Jacob to convinced him to work here at the Lucky Lady."

"Great, a good a steak sounds mighty fine about now," said Brian with a slight grin upon his lips.

"Of course the steaks--- just then the conversation at the table nearest the bar got quite a bit louder. There were three men sitting at the table and the loud voices were coming from the two that were sitting across from each other. They were so loud the rest of the saloon's customers were silent, and all heads were turned toward their table. The two men arguing paid no attention. They were only focused upon their argument.

"How can you say that?" shouted the man on the farthest side of the table, "I've been working that section of the stream for two weeks!"

"Two weeks, ha! I've been working that claim for the past three days!" roared the man across from him.

"Not true!" screamed the first man, " Until I came to town tonight, to pick up supplies, I've been at the site for two straight weeks and I hadn't seen a soul that entire time!"

"Mister you're dreamin'!" replied the second man, shaking his finger at the man across from him. "I've been there and had some luck, and now you want to horn in on my find!

"Liar!" shrieked the first man, shoving his chair back, standing up, and drawing his pistol from the holster on his hip.

The second man drew his own pistol and fired a shot just as he brought his pistol above the top of the table. The first man staggered back from the impact of the bullet hitting just below his sternum. A look of surprise spread slowly across his face, and the pistol dropped from his fingers to the floor. After taking a step forward, he slumped across the table then slid off and thudded onto the floor.

Sheriff Baker was on his feet in an instant with pistol drawn. He said to the man sitting at the table, "Don't move!"

The man who had fired the shot froze. Everyone in the saloon followed suit remaining still waiting for the sheriff's next command.

"Slowly--- place your pistol on the table than raise your hands above your head." ordered Sheriff Baker.

The man extended his hand with the pistol toward the table and set it down as smoothly as possible. He then gingerly raised both hands above his head.

Baker speaking out of the corner of his mouth barked toward the bar," Jacob come get this pistol for me!"

Jacob swiftly emerged from around the counter, moved to the table and grabbed the pistol.

"Sheriff it was in self-defense," said the man sitting with raised hands. Before responding the sheriff said to Brian, "Brian will you check the injured man?"

Brian got up from his seat and kneeled down next to the man lying on the floor. While Brian checked the wounded miner the man that had shot him said, "You all saw it, He was going to shoot me. I had to defend myself."

"Be quiet!" directed Sheriff Baker, "You'll get your chance to speak. For now don't say a word, and don't move." Then speaking to Brian, "How is he?"

"I think he's had it," answered Brian lifting his ear off the man's chest, "He isn't breathing and I couldn't hear a heartbeat."

"Okay---John, go get the doc," said Baker to the smaller of the two men standing at the bar.

" Sure thing sheriff." responded the man after downing the last of the drink in his hand. Placing the glass on the counter he dashed through the swinging doors into the street. To the other man at the bar Baker said, "Willie go find Jasper and have him come here right away."

"Yes Sheriff," he replied and followed John out the door.

Sheriff Baker returned his attention to the man at the table with his hands still in the air though they had slumped to the level of his eyes.

"You can put your hands down now," said Baker.

The man lowered his hands and put them in his lap. Sheriff Baker stepped so that he was facing the man. " I'm not going to refute that you had the right to defend yourself but I am concerned how fast you were willing to use your gun, particularly in this instance."

"He drew on me. I was afraid he was going to shoot me," said the man calmly.

"That may be true, but from my vantage point he wasn't going to use his gun," said Baker with doubt in his voice.

"That's because you weren't on the barrel end of it," said the man shrugging his shoulders.

"We're not going to get anywhere debating about it here. I'm going to take you to the sheriff's office and will discuss it there," stated Sheriff Baker.

"Okay whatever you say, but all these witnesses will back me up that it was self- defense."

The conversation stopped for a moment. Brian was still kneeling next to the victim on the floor when out of the corner of his eye he thought he noticed the Sheriff give a slight nod of his head to the man that had fired the shot. It was so slight that he wasn't sure if he had really seen it. He wouldn't have given it a second thought except it looked as though the man that had fired the shot gave a similar nod in return.

Just then Jasper burst through the door, paused as he studied the scene in the saloon then walked over to the Sheriff. Looking at the apparent dead man on the floor Jasper said, "Willie told me what happened--- what's next?"

"I'm going to take this fellow over to the office and question him some more," answered Sheriff Baker, pointing to the man that did the shooting. "When the doc gets here have him take a look at the man on the floor. If he's dead, take care of the body. If he's still alive help the doc get him over to his place."

"Okay Sheriff," said Jasper.

Sheriff Baker then directed the shooter to head toward the entrance of the saloon. The man slowly got up from his chair and made his way to the swinging doors followed by Sheriff Baker. A moment later the town doctor entered through the door and Jasper had him examine the man on the floor. The doctor quickly determined that the man was indeed dead. Standing up he talked to the deputy and explained what he wanted done with the body. Jasper then called over two of the men standing amongst the other patrons of the saloon and directed them to take the body with the doctor. The two men lifted the dead miner off the floor one holding him under his armpits while the other grasped his ankles.

Once they had left the saloon the deputy ordered the rest to get back to their business and to not be surprised if they were contacted later to give their account of the incident. Turning to Brian who had been standing near the deputy, he said, "You certainly have been introduced to the worst Buffalo Gap can offer with what happened outside of town earlier today and now this."

"Not what I had expected, that's for sure," said Brian in agreement.

"Well, hopefully tomorrow begins better, “said Jasper encouragingly. "Is there anything I can do for you now?" he offered.

"You could point me in the direction of your hotel or whatever type of lodging establishment you have here in town. I think I've had enough for one day."

"Sure thing. Step through those doors turn right and three buildings down you'll see "Hotel" written in big black letters. Nothing fancy but you'll find a comfortable bed for the night."

"Thanks. I appreciate it," said Brian heading toward the doors, "See you tomorrow," he added with a two-finger salute off the brim of his hat.

As he walked through the swinging doors, Brian couldn't get the look he'd seen between the sheriff and the man that had done the shooting out of his mind.

Chapter 5

The morning was getting warmer now that the sun had been up for several hours. When Sarah and the soldiers had first risen and fixed a breakfast of beans and bacon there was a chill in the air. There wasn't frost on the ground but as cold as it felt to the small troop from Fort Meade, there might as well have been. After a quick breakfast, Lieutenant Carlson had his men break camp, and the small detachment was soon on the trail to Buffalo Gap.

The lieutenant figured they would reach town somewhere around ten or eleven that morning if all went smoothly. Whatever had caused the disturbance outside the camp didn't recur which allowed for a somewhat peaceful night. Of course, as leader of the group Lieutenant Carlson couldn't totally relax. It was his responsibility to get them safely to the mining town. Under normal circumstances this would have been a simple assignment. However, the discovery of gold in the Black Hills, along with the agreement the US government had made with the local Indians, made keeping white people out of the mountains nearly impossible.

The government was finding out rapidly that the greed for quick riches was too great for the common citizen to care for the rights of the local native population. The flow of whites into the area had been gradually increasing as the word of gold had spread throughout the country. This only intensified the clashes between the Lakota and those who were illegally within the boundaries set by the treaty. The army was caught in the middle having to protect the rights of the treaty of 1868, while also protecting the lives of American citizens that were moving into the Black Hills region.

Lieutenant Carlson didn't care much for the politics of the situation, he just knew it made his duty more difficult trying to please both sides. There were renegade bands of Lakota that attacked those they felt had infringed upon the treaty, and this included the US army. So as they traveled the final miles to Buffalo Gap he was uneasy in his saddle knowing they were going through disputed Lakota territory.

As he passed the wagon on his way to the front of the column Sarah greeted the lieutenant with a good morning and a pleasant smile upon her face. The lieutenant tipped his hat in response and slowed his horse to keep pace with the wagon when Sarah said, "Beautiful morning wouldn't you agree lieutenant?"

Scanning the prairie before them he answered, "Yes ma'am, it truly is a gorgeous morning."

Sarah took a deep breath and let it out slowly, then said light heartedly, "Everything is so fresh and clean it makes one feel free and alive," then with a dourer tone, she added, "Back in Harrisburg, I always felt penned in with all the buildings and all the people rushing here and there."

"There's plenty of space to lose one's self out here in the Dakotas. But you have to be careful the prairie can be inhospitable. The weather can change at the drop of a hat and the winters can be quite severe." cautioned Lieutenant Carlson.

"That may be so, but for the moment this could be considered God's country," quipped Sarah as she swept her outstretched arm in a gentle arc.

"Ma'am, once again I agree with you. At this particular time of year the Black Hills have a beauty all their own."

The two became silent as they surveyed the landscape before them. The warmth of the sun upon their faces and a hint of breeze comforted them both as they travelled through the lush rustling grass that stretched into the distance on both sides of the valley they were following.

Sarah broke the silence with another question," How long until we reach Buffalo Gap?"

The Lieutenant stood up in his stirrups to stretch his legs and answered, "If we have no trouble the rest of the way, we should arrive around ten."

"I pray all goes well then," said Sarah with a smile.

Lieutenant Carlson responded by tipping his hat once again, and then tapped his horse with the heels of his boots and galloped up to the front of the column. He stayed at the front guiding the detachment southward over the rolling land that butted up against the ridges forming the eastern boundary of the Black Hills. Periodically Carlson would ride up and down the column to make sure all was in order as they traveled toward Buffalo Gap. As it turned out, the going was good and the tiny group made decent time. They did, indeed, reach the outskirts of Buffalo gap well before noon.

Coming into town from the north, they soon reached the office of the Buffalo Mining Company. Lieutenant Carlson signaled to Private Henderson to bring the wagon next to the sidewalk in front of the office and wait. Henderson did so while the rest of the soldiers guided their horses up to the railing near the wagon. Carlson then ordered his men to dismount and be at ease, while he and Sarah went into the mining company's office to meet with Mr. Langston.

As Carlson was getting down from his horse Sam Henderson jumped from the wagon and offered to help Sarah from the wagon. Even though she didn't really need help, she politely accepted Henderson's offer, and allowed him to aid her off the wagon and onto the ground. Turning, she reached into the bed of the wagon and grabbed her dust covered travel bag that had been packed behind the seat. With bag in hand, she walked around the back of the wagon to the Buffalo Mining Company's door where she waited for Lieutenant Carlson.

The Lieutenant tied his horse to the railing next to the wagon and joined Sarah on the sidewalk. Taking off his gloves, he gripped the doorknob, pushed the door open, then stepped back and waited for Sarah to enter the building. She thanked him with a smile, then pushed the door gently and entered. The Lieutenant immediately followed and closed the door behind them.

Sitting at the table next to the roll top desk were Mr. Langston and Brian Dolan. Langston looked toward the two as they entered while Brian turned in his chair so that he could see who was entering the office. Langston jumped to his feet and came swiftly around the table. Holding out his hand he said exuberantly, "Ah, Sarah! You're finally here!"

Langston seized her hand with both of his, and shook it heartily.

"It's good to see you, Uncle, "acknowledged Sarah as her uncle continued to shake her hand.

"I've been looking forward to seeing you too," answered Langston. He let go of her hand as he guided her into the room. "You must be tired after your long journey. Please, come sit down." he urged as he led her to the empty seat next to Brian.

"Thanks, but I 'm fine I ---"

"No, I insist. What manners would I be showing if I allowed you to remain standing?" said Langston. Sarah didn't resist his urging and sat quietly in the chair he offered.

"It's good to see you Sarah. What has it been, three years?" said Langston.

"Yes, just a little over three years," agreed Sarah.

"Well, you haven't changed a bit, just as pretty as ever," stated Langston with a big grin on his face. But the grin quickly disappeared and was replaced with a shocked look. "Excuse me, I talk about manners, but I haven't made introductions. Sarah, this is Brian Dolan. Brian, my niece Sarah Schuler."

Sarah turned to face Brian.

"Mr. Dolan, I'm pleased to meet you. I know your name from when you worked with my uncle in New York."

"It is a pleasure to finally meet you miss Schuler. Your uncle spoke of you several times while we were in New York." said Brian politely.

Brian thought back to those conversations as he studied the face of the girl next to him. Langston had mentioned her on several occasions but his description of Sarah during those conversations fell way short of the loveliness that sat before him now. Just then Langston interrupted his thoughts with his booming voice, "Sarah how was the trip from Pennsylvania?

"Overall, it's been quite pleasant. The country out here is beautiful and Lieutenant Carlson and his men have treated me with the greatest of care and kindness," responded Sarah.

"Glad to hear it. I am truly sorry your mother wasn't able to come. How is she doing?" said Langston with concern in his tone.

"Well as expected, considering, " answered Sarah clasping her hands together on her lap, "she has good days and bad, but her bad days haven't gotten worse."

"Thank heaven for that," then turning toward the open door at the back of the office Langston shouted," Jim---Jim come out here!"

After a short pause Jim stepped through the door.

"Yes Mr. Langston." he inquired.

"I'm sure my niece is tired from her travels and for that matter she may be hungry. Jim, would you please escort her to the hotel and get her a room? I'll be there by noon to take you to lunch," pausing then looking back at Sarah with a smile on his face, "Is that agreeable?

"Thank you, that would be nice." replied Sarah.

"Wonderful!" exclaimed Langston then motioning to Jim, he said "Jim, if you would take her and her things now."

Jim immediately scurried over to Sarah, picked up her travel bag on the floor next to her chair, and held his arm toward the front door. Sarah stood up from her chair and walked forward. Lieutenant Carlson met her at the door, opening it for them as they exited into the street. Carlson then closed the door, and walked over to where Langston and Dolan were at the table. Langston moved back behind the table and sat down.

"Lieutenant, Brian Dolan here is my new foreman up in the mine fields. We go back to when I was in New York and I believe he will do a good job for us here in the Black Hills."

"Mr. Dolan," acknowledged Carlson with a nod.

"Lieutenant," responded Brian matter-of-factly.

"You've come at the right time Bill. Some of the mines are producing well and we have a good size shipment for you to take back to Fort Meade," said Langston seriously.

"How much this time?" asked Bill.

"A little over eighty-three thousand dollars," replied Langston, "with that amount do you think you have enough men to protect it while traveling to Fort Meade? "

"Whee! I would say the mines are producing, " concurred Carlson emphatically then inquired, " Who knows how much gold is going with us?"

"There is just myself, Jim and Brian," answered Langston.

"We have seven," said Carlson stroking his bottom lip with his index finger and thumb then added, "I think that should be enough especially since we are military, that in itself should deter any who might think about stealing the gold."

"Good, I 'm going to send Brian and Jim with you---at least part of the way, before they head into the Black Hills. Brian needs to get to the mines to familiarize himself with the operation, and I'm having Jim go along to show him the way. That will give you two more men," said Langston.

"We'll take all the help you want to provide," said Carlson with genuine appreciation in his tone.

"When do you want to head back?" asked Langston.

"Normally I would head back this afternoon, but with the type of cargo we are carrying I want to be on the trail as few nights as possible. We'll get an early start tomorrow morning," replied Carlson.

"Let's meet here at six tomorrow and we'll load the wagon then," directed Langston.

"Six then," said Carlson. He then gave a semi salute to Langston who responded by getting up from his chair. The Lieutenant then turned to Brian, gave a similar salute, and then turned on his heel and headed toward the door. As he was exiting, Langston spoke to Brian, "I have a lunch date with my niece, Mr. Dolan, you are welcome to join us."

Without hesitation Brian responded, " I would be more than happy to join you."

"Excellent!" said Langston with his ever-prevalent smile.

On the way over to the hotel the two men spoke of the preparations for transferring the gold to the wagon in the morning. Virgil told Brian that he could be at the office to help if he wanted, but that it wasn't really necessary because Lieutenant Carlson and his men would provide plenty of manpower to get the gold into the wagon within a short amount of time. He emphasized that Brian needed to be ready to leave with the soldiers just after dawn. Brian indicated that he would be there early enough to help with the loading of the wagon. He also let Langston know he was eager to get to the minefields and check out the operation first hand.

Upon reaching the hotel their conversation turned to Langston's niece and Brian was glad to talk about the young lady from Pennsylvania. Entering the lobby of the hotel the two men found themselves alone, as there wasn't even a clerk behind the reception desk. The two continued to discuss Sarah as they waited for someone from the hotel to enter the lobby. Langston was reminding Brian how he, Langston, had met Sarah, Sarah's mother and Sarah's aunt.

Just then a man that look to be in his late fifties with a head showing the beginnings of balding and a bushy mustache that matched the gray color of his hair entered the lobby through a door to Langston and Dolan's left.

"Mr. Langston. Welcome and a good morning to ya," said the man as he walked behind the reception counter.

"A good morning to you as well," said Langston moving up to the counter. Langston then introduced Brian to Phil Simpson, the proprietor of the hotel. The two exchanged pleasantries and Phil turned his attention to Langston and said, "You must be here to see your niece."

"That would be correct," answered Langston, "We are here to have lunch with her."

"Wonderful. I'll take you into the dining room and you can have the table of your choice," said Phil.

"Phil take Brian into the dining room and he can pick the table. I'm going to go up and see if Sarah is ready." Putting a hand on Brian's shoulder he said to Brian, "I won't be long." Then to Phil he asked, "Which room?"

"Room C."

Langston then headed up the stairs just to the left of the reception desk. Phil motioned to Brian to follow him and the two of them went into the dining room. There were four tables spaced at regular distances throughout the room. Each table was covered with a white tablecloth and in the middle of each table was a small vase with daisies. Brian scanned the tables and decided on the one nearest to him. Phil invited Brian to take a seat while he went to pick up their menus.

Brian placed his hat on one of the two pegs of the chair he pulled from the table and sat down. Looking about him he noticed the dining room was furnished simply, which gave it a home like feeling. Phil had gone over to a table next to the door that Brian assumed led to the kitchen. There he snatched up a couple of menus and brought them over to the table. He gave one to Brian and laid the other on the table in front of the chair directly to Brian's left.

"You'll find we don't have a great selection, but what we do serve is quite good," said Baker with a touch of pride.

After studying the menu for a moment Brian replied, "Everything looks inviting especially after eating my own cooking since leaving Pine Ridge."

"Anything to drink while you wait?

"No thanks. I'll wait until Mr. Langston and his niece join me."

"Of course," acknowledged Mr. Baker. Then changing the subject, he asked, "Will you be in Buffalo Gap long?

"I expect for a while," answered Brian, " Mr. Langston just hired me on as foreman for the Company's operation at the mines."

"Is that a fact?" said Simpson with a slight surprise in his voice.

At that moment Langston and Sarah enter the dining room, and seeing Brian, Langston led Sarah over to the table. Sarah thanked her uncle as he held her chair for her, "Hello again, Mr. Dolan." she said.

"Miss," nodded Brian then handing her a menu added, "I hope you are hungry. The menu has some mouth-watering items."

"Hungry? Yes, I could eat a horse," replied Sarah.

"Order what you want, you're my guest---you too, Brian," advised Langston.

The three then diligently studied their menus and when Phil returned to the table a few moments later, they placed their order. Once the requests were given Sarah asked her uncle," So uncle Virgil why did you invite my mother to come visit you here in Buffalo Gap?"

"Whoa! That was direct and to the point," Langston said with amusement.

"Well there were many letters from you over the past several years. Then, when we received an invitation out of the blue to a place in the wilds of the Dakota Territory, we were very curious to hear your reason, "said Sarah pointedly.

"Fair enough," admitted Langston without argument, "you and your mother deserve an explanation. As you know, things didn't turn out for the best when I went to New York after marrying your aunt. Things went well financially, and I have never forgiven myself for not coming back to Pennsylvania sooner when Caroline became ill. Your mother was the only one in your family that treated me with kindness, even after her sister died. Finding myself in a position of some success, I feel I owe it to your family to share in that success. This time I didn't want to wait until it was too late. I wanted your mother to see what we had accomplished here and to be a part of it."

"If I may be so bold, what is this success you speak of, and what part would my mother play in it?" asked Sarah.

Langston pulled a pocket watch from his vest pocket scrutinized the face of it then spoke, " You may know that just to the north of us are the Black Hills. When gold was discovered, I was fortunate to get a claim early that contained a fair amount of gold. With that early return I was able to establish the Buffalo Mining Company and extend my interest into managing other claims of other miners. Soon the company had enough capital to modernize this trading post size town into what you saw as you rode in this morning. The gold in the Black Hills doesn't look to dry up anytime soon, so I see our interest in this area continuing to grow." Langston motioned to Phil and then finished his answer to his niece, "Your mother's part in all this well---I think it would be better to show you what I have in mind than to try and explain it here."

" All right uncle, you have caught my interest, and I will try to be patient until you show me how this involves my family," said Sarah not totally satisfied with her uncle's answer.

Phil appeared next to the table and Langston ordered coffee to be brought with their meals. The conversation of the three throughout the rest of the meal consisted of Langston describing how he came to the area and his initial frustration at not finding gold. Then he accidently came across the first signs that led to a rich vein of gold that began it all. He then told how he used his early earnings to build up Buffalo Gap and how he encouraged others from back east to come to the area. The word got out, and within eight months the population of Buffalo Gap had quadrupled and the number of claims in the Black Hills had tripled with a few of them giving up enough gold to make some rich.

Langston also related the difficulties he and the others had faced because of the treaty with the Lakota. There had been numerous skirmishes with the neighboring Indians that had resulted in deaths on both sides. But, as Langston explained, it had been worth the risk so far because of the potential the Black Hills had shown. This topic of conversation continued throughout their meal with both Sarah and Brian asking questions periodically, Langston was enthusiastically willing to answer each one.

Toward the end of lunch, the conversation turned to the next day. Langston reminded Brian when to be in front of his office in the morning. Jim and Brian would help escort the wagon and its cargo until they reached the trail that branched off toward the mines where they would leave the cavalry detachment. This pricked the interest of Sarah and she said, "With everything centered around the mines and the production of gold, I would like to go along. I hope that wouldn't be too much of an imposition."

"I'm not sure that would be wise," responded Langston with concern in his tone, "it's pretty rough out there."

"Your uneasiness is understandable, but I do believe I can handle myself appropriately," said Sarah confidently, "and besides this will allow me to get an idea of the mining end of your business first hand."

Her uncle didn't seem convinced from the look on his face but after some thought he asked Brian, "What do you think, Brian. Should I allow her to go along?"

"Normally, I would be against bringing a woman, especially one that has just arrived from the east coast, to a mining camp. But in the short amount of time I've been around this young lady, I have little doubt that she can handle herself adequately," replied Brian as he looked in Sarah's direction with a friendly smile.

"I guess you are here to see all that we do. Okay, be in front of my office by 6:00 tomorrow morning and you can go along," agreed Langston with some reluctance.

"I look forward to it," said Sarah eagerly.

Chapter 6

Brian felt slightly out of place as he rode along the trail heading north towards Fort Meade. Not that it was a negative feeling, quite the opposite. He had been traveling on his own most of the time in the past year, and being here with a small group of people was refreshing. Not to say he didn't enjoy the solitude of traveling by himself, but having someone to talk to now and again was a treat, he realized now, that he had missed. In particular when that someone was a pleasant and engaging female.

The morning had begun for Brian just after the sun had shown itself above the eastern horizon. He had arrived at the appointed time to help with the loading of the gold from the various mines to the north of Buffalo Gap. The town's central location made it easy to collect and then transport each shipment north to Fort Meade on its way to the east coast.

The loading of the gold had gone smoothly and all those travelling with the Army detachment were ready to travel, including Sarah Schuler and Jim Paxton. After loading the wagon, the soldiers and their civilian companions headed north back along the trail they had taken down from Fort Meade two days before. The troop fell into the same positions they had occupied when coming south, with Lieutenant Carlson at the head of the column most of the time. Sarah was on horseback since she would be on the trail with Brian and Jim when they spilt off to go to the mines. Her uncle had a horse waiting for her that morning and the two took to each other right away. Sarah couldn't say the same for her riding though. It had been sometime since she had been in the saddle and it took a good portion of the early morning to become comfortable again.

Once she settled into traveling on horseback, Sarah was able to enjoy the beauty of the early summer prairie with the Black Hills off in the distance. The grasses were green and stretched endlessly to the east over rolling hills. After the few days Sarah had spent in this open country, she understood why many from the east coast had a difficult time adjusting to living in territories such as the Dakotas and Montana. There was so much space and for many farmers the nearest neighbor or town could be several miles away. Not like the big cities along the coast, where civilization offered its culture and entertainment abundantly.

Brian interrupted Sarah's thoughts as he brought his horse up alongside hers.

"How are you doing?" said Brian.

Stretching her back straight then relaxing, Sarah said, "Doing much better, now that I've had time in the saddle. That first hour was a bit uncomfortable."

"Wait until tomorrow," chuckled Brian, "

"What do you mean?" asked Sarah.

"You may have been slightly uncomfortable this morning, but tomorrow, my guess is your bottom is going to be a bit sore," explained Brian.

Sarah remained silent, pondering what Brian had just told her. "I guess there are things one has to deal with good or bad when venturing away from home, "she smiled.

"That's a pretty positive outlook considering you're a city girl."

"What makes you think I'm a city girl?" demanded Sarah gently.

"I just assumed that being from the east coast, you must live in one of the big cities," said Brian calmly.

"You're half right. I grew up in Harrisburg, Pennsylvania, but it was outside the city limits so I experienced both city life and country life. My father made sure I learned to ride and shoot along with the proper etiquette of being a lady," responded Sarah, with a touch of defensiveness.

"I stand corrected," said Brian.

The two became silent each looking straight ahead as they rode together. After a minute, Brian attempted to take the conversation in a different direction as he motioned with his hand, "What do you think of the Dakota Territory?"

Sarah considered the rolling hills off to her right then spoke, "The open grass land of the Dakotas is quite beautiful, at least this time of the year. But, I have observed as I traveled farther west from Harrisburg the wildness of the country relates with the wildness of its people."

"How do you mean?"

"For one thing, I saw a lowering of moral standards the farther west I traveled," explained Sarah.

"Is that so," said Brian nudging his horse closer to Sarah's horse, "and what standard do you hold to?"

"God's word found in the Holy Bible," replied Sarah plainly.

"God's word you say. And you believe everything that is written in the Bible?" questioned Brian.

"I believe the Bible is the inspired word of God," returned Sarah.

"Why do you believe in the Bible? Where is the proof?" prodded Brian.

"I believe the Lord through His grace saved me, which gives me faith in Him and His word," answered Sarah.

"What standards does your bible give for the folks of this earth?" asked Brian with true interest.

"Well, that is a question that doesn't have a simple answer. I can say this though; first of all, there is the example of Christ throughout the Bible. Being sinless, He is one we should strive to imitate. Secondly, there are many passages that discuss and explain the difference between right and wrong. One such passage can be found in Romans Chapter one, particularly verse 28 through verse 32," said Sarah.

"How often do you refer to these words of the Bible," inquired Brian.

"I try to read it every---Suddenly the crack of a rifle rang from Brian's and Sarah's left. Brian instinctively crouched over his horse's neck. As he did so he saw one of the soldiers riding in front of the wagon slump off his horse. Then more gunfire exploded from the direction of the first shot. Another soldier lurched forward in his saddle, but kept from falling off by grabbing the front of the saddle. The horse startled by the soldier's sudden pitch onto its neck bolted to the right off the trail.

Brian, recovering from his initial surprise, snatched the reins of Sarah's horse and kicked his own horse into a gallop. They rode to the right of the trail and away from the shooting. He then furtively searched the area in front and to his right for any means of cover or escape from the gunfire. The spot for the ambush had been chosen well. The right side of the trail had no trees to provide cover for the troops, but to the left there was a grove of ponderosa pine about seventy-five yards from the trail. Giving plenty of cover for the attacking party to spring their trap and hide behind once the bullets began to fly.

Fortunately, there were several large boulders jutting up from the prairie floor, large enough to hide behind. This is where Brian guided the two horses. As they were making their dash to the protection of the rocks, Brian heard Lieutenant Carlson barking orders to his men to take cover and return fire. The soldiers had been well trained; they had already regained their composer after the opening attack and were firing into the grove of trees.

Lieutenant Carlson then directed Private Henderson to get the wagon over next to the rocks and take cover behind them. Henderson responded instantly and drove the wagon next to the nearest boulder and vigorously pulled on the reins bringing the wagon to an abrupt stop. Henderson scooped up his carbine from the floor of the buckboard and leaped from the seat over the boulder and onto the ground. He immediately leaned against the boulder and looked for a target.

Bullets began to splatter and ricochet off the rocks Brian and Sarah had taken refuge behind. All of the soldiers, except for the one that had been shot from his horse, had taken cover behind the same boulders. The large rocks were the only concealment available. Whether the large stones have broken off of the Black Hills and rolled to their present position or they are the remains of years of weathering from wind and rain is anybody's guess. The fact that the stones were there at all was all that mattered to the eight-people hiding behind them for protection from the vicious onslaught of rifle fire from the trees across the trail.

All the soldiers and civilians alike had dismounted and taken position against the rocks. As each man found the protection of the boulders and positioned himself against the rocks the return fire from the boulders increased in intensity. Lieutenant Carlson saw however, that this haphazard shooting wouldn't work for long. Shouting above the din of the gunfire he ordered all to cease-fire. Once all had complied he said with a firm voice, "Men take your time, pick your target and make each shot count. We need to conserve our ammunition until we know for sure what we are up against."

Private Marshal located to the right of Lieutenant Carlson uttered, "Sir, what about Ridley? He's taken one in the belly."

Lieutenant Carlson looked in the direction Marshal was pointing. Sitting up against a boulder Private Ridley had his two hands one on top of the other pressed against his stomach just below the rib cage. His hands and shirt were stained with blood and the grimace on his face revealed the wound was painful. Darting over to the wounded soldier Carlson took a quick look at the wound and saw that the bullet had entered from the side and exited through the front at a forty-five-degree angle. The bullet didn't seem to have hit any vital organ it just left a nasty hole.

Looking up from the wounded soldier Carlson quickly scanned around. Spotting Sarah he cried," Miss Schuler over here quick!"

Sarah responded immediately. In a crouch she scurried to the side of the Lieutenant and kneeled beside the wounded man. Carlson took the kerchief from around his neck shook it and folded it twice into a square, which he then placed on Ridley's wound. Turning to Sarah he said, "Miss Schuler if you could tend to this man's wound that would be a great help. If you would just keep pressure on the kerchief to prevent any more blood lost, he'll be okay."

Without hesitating, Sarah stepped over Ridley's outstretched legs and knelt down, placing her hand gently on the kerchief.

"I've got it Lieutenant," said Sarah firmly, "I'll see to it he is well looked after. If some water could be brought that would be appreciated." Sarah then focused her attention completely on the injured soldier.

Lieutenant Carlson gave the appropriate order for water to be brought to Miss Schuler then he returned his attention to the battle. The concentration of fire coming from the trees had not slackened since the opening attack. The bullets continued non-stop slapping the boulders or zipping above the heads of those hiding behind them. The soldiers, on the other hand, had heeded the command of their lieutenant by being patient and taking a shot when they saw a definite target.

Once Brian had led Sarah to safety behind the boulders, he snatched his Winchester, dismounted, and found a good spot up against the rocks in which to fire back. He was grateful to have his repeating rifle as opposed to the soldiers and their single shot carbines. They may have better accuracy at farther distances but he was glad to have the fifteen-shot capability before having to reload.

Looking down his barrel he tried to get a fix on any of those that were firing from across the trail. Scanning the trees he saw several bodies lean from behind the protection of the trunks, fire their weapon, and then pull back behind the tree. He noticed one particular ambusher just off to his left being quite bold. He exposed himself much more than did any of the others as he took his shots. Brian lined up the sights of his rifle on the open area just to the left of the tree the ambusher was hiding behind and waited. The ambusher didn't disappoint, within seconds he popped his body from behind the tree and took a shot. Brian held his own fire, he wanted to make sure when he did fire it counted. Sure enough within ten seconds the shooter moved from behind the tree took a shot and quickly moved back.

Brian again withheld from firing. He used these two times to study the man's position as he came from behind the tree. The next time the man showed himself Brian would be ready. Several seconds later the shooter leaned from the tree and Brian fired. At seventy yards with his rifle resting on the rock in front of him and the size of the target, Brian's shot was not difficult. The bullet hit the man just below the neck driving him back from the tree where he collapsed to the ground. Brian watched for any movement. After several seconds the body remained still, and Brian searched for another target.

The grove of pine trees was so thick that the number of ambushers within its cover was difficult for the soldiers to determine. But by the rate and amount of fire Lieutenant Carlson believed that there were at least ten gunmen hiding amongst the trees. Moving back and forth behind his men, the lieutenant was able to direct the defense of his small party effectively giving encouragement when necessary and instruction when needed. Just as he started back, Private Dixon who was the last man on the right tumbled back from his firing position landing on his back clutching his neck.

The lieutenant instantly dropped to his knee next to the wounded soldier. Blood was gushing from where the bullet had entered through the trachea just above the Adams apple and from the back of his neck where the bullet had exited. Lieutenant Carlson slammed his palms down onto Dixon's throat trying to exert enough pressure to halt the bleeding. Dixon convulsed and gurgled. The lieutenant's effort helped slow the flow of blood, but the stream of blood coming from the back of the neck continued unabated. Then it was over. Private Dixon's body relaxed and the convulsions ceased.

Carlson took his hands away from Dixon's neck and let them drop to his side. For a moment he just looked into the face of the young man.

His shoulders slumped and he felt helpless. Wishing he had done more, but knowing that he had done all that he could, he slowly stood up and turned back to the battle raging behind him. Seeing the rest of his troop continuing to combat the enemy his mind was drawn quickly back to the crisis at hand. He immediately stepped down the line to access the situation and give the necessary orders to keep up a good defense.

Just as he passed a crevice between two boulders a bullet fragment ricocheted off the nearest boulder and caught him in the right shoulder. The impact caused him to spin to his right, more out of surprise, then from the force of the fragment entering his shoulder. The piece of bullet didn't penetrate to deeply and after examining it briefly, he decided it could wait. He resumed his advance down the line.

Coming up to sergeant Halsey he said in a hushed voice, "We just lost Dixon."

Keeping his eyes toward the grove of pine trees Halsey responded, "Tough break, he just arrived about three weeks ago."

"That brings our number down to seven, actually six, with Ridley's wound he's not much help."

"We can't afford to lose anyone else." stated Halsey, firing a shot, then quickly ejecting the spent cartridge and placing a fresh one in the breech of his carbine.

"Holding them off until dark is a tall order since there's about nine or ten hours of daylight left. We could try and out run them on the horses riding into the prairie but that would mean leaving the gold, and I'm not ready to do that just yet," said Carlson.

"We don't even really know what we're up against, how many they are, or who they are," said Halsey flatly with a touch of frustration in his voice.

"Well, one thing we know for sure is---they're after the gold shipment," returned Carlson as he peeked over the boulder in the direction of the ambushers. As he scanned the trees he observed another of the attackers fall from behind one of the trees off to the right. *That will help some,* thought Carlson. He looked to his right down the boulder to see who might have fired the fatal shot. Most likely it was Private Hastings. It was definitely not Mr. Paxton. He was sitting with his back against the boulder chin on his chest with his hands covering his ears. "Useless," thought Lieutenant Carlson disgustedly. Another prim and proper Jim Dandy from the east coast with no backbone.

"Sir!" yelled Private Hastings, "Look off to the right coming out of the trees!"

Carlson looked in the direction Hastings indicated and saw three men on horseback riding away from the grove of trees on a course that would bring them parallel with the defenders' right flank.

"It looks like they are trying to get around behind us," said Carlson

"It looks like they are trying to do the same thing to our left," said Sergeant Halsey.

Three riders were moving in a similar route off to the left of the defenders. The firing from the trees increased. The ambushers were attempting to keep the heads of the defenders down so they could not fire on the riders moving around both flanks.

Crouched below the rim of the boulder Brian shouted to Lieutenant Carlson, "What do you suggest, Lieutenant?"

The lieutenant looked to his left, then to the trees, then to his right. Seeing all that was unfolding before him he did not have a good answer to Brian's question.

Chapter 7

Brian looked to his right past the boulders and saw the three ambushers spread out from each other as they reached a point that brought them behind the boulders protecting the defenders. When they were approximately ten yards apart, they halted their horses and dismounted. Looking quickly to his left Brian observed the riders were doing the same thing. In a few moments, the attackers would have them in a cross fire and there was nowhere to hide.

"Brian, you and Sam take those to our left!" cried Lieutenant Carlson. Swinging about, he hollered to Marshal, " Austin, you and I have those to our right!

The four men opened fired on the new threats coming from each side of their perimeter. The men were so keen on getting lead down range that their aim was erratic. Dirt kicked up all around the six dismounted riders. They hastily returned fired with no more accuracy than the soldiers and Brian had shown with their volley.

Brian had another cartridge loaded instantly in his lever action rifle. His second shot was headed down range before the other three had completed locking the 45-70 cartridges into the receiver of their rifles. This time, Brian's shot found its target. The middle rider fell forward clutching his left leg as the bullet tore into his thigh just above the kneecap. The other two riders kept firing and with repeating rifles of their own they were slapping the ground repeatedly around Brian and Sam.

Suddenly, out from the edge of the grove of trees Brian saw five new riders coming hard toward the three ambushers. As they drew near to the gunman, Brian realized the riders were Indians. Their attention was fully focused on the three ambushers and when they had closed to within fifty yards, the two that had rifles opened fired. The ambushers were caught totally unawares and didn't respond at first. Then the truth of the matter sunk in and the two uninjured men scrambled to their horses and clambered with difficulty into their saddles. The injured man tried desperately to hobble over to his horse but his damaged leg impeded his progress.

Before the men were completely in the saddle, the Indians were upon them. The nearest ambusher was knocked from his horse by a savage blow to his head from the swing of a stone war club. He hit the ground and didn't move. A second Lakota had charged his horse directly to the injured ambusher, and while the animal was still moving, slid from its back and dashed to the man with knife drawn. The ambusher made a feeble attempt to raise his rifle to defend himself but the Lakota easily pushed the rifle aside and drove his knife into the chest of the man. The man's eyes opened wide from the impact, and he fell on his back to the ground with the Indian on top of him.

The third ambusher had climbed into his saddle quicker than his partner choosing to drop his rifle just as he got to his horse. He now kicked his horse hard yelling as he did so causing the horse to take off into the prairie at top speed. The last three Lakota with high-pitched yelps were after him and they narrowed the distance in short order. Just as they were getting to within a few feet, the fleeing ambusher began to pull away. The rider's horse was strong and rested giving it the power to begin putting some distance between themselves and their pursuers. But the Lakota were experienced in this type of chase and did not waver in their pursuit.

The lead Lakota had his bow and arrow at the ready, this was just like so many Buffalo hunts before. With legs held tightly to the horse's side he took aim and let his arrow fly. At the short distance, the arrow found the ambusher just below the right shoulder blade. The rider flinched as the arrow pierced his skin and entered the muscle. He fought to hold the reins and was able to keep up the horse's speed separating himself further from his pursuers. After another hundred yards the Lakota knew they couldn't keep up so they stopped their pursuit, watched the rider and his horse disappear over a knoll, then headed back to the battle.

Back at the trail a similar scene had unfolded out beyond the boulders to the right of the defenders. Another group of Lakota had overtaken the three men trying to out flank the group behind the rocks and in short order neutralized the threat. At the same time the firing from the grove of trees came to a sudden stop replaced by screaming and yelling.

Suddenly a man burst from the tree line running madly in the direction of the boulders across the trail. This was followed directly by another man, a Lakota, dashing from the same place. Before the first man out of the trees was halfway to the trail, the Lakota had caught up with him and swinging his war club caught the man squarely in the back of the head. The man went down hard rolling several times before stopping face down. The Lakota rapidly closed the distance between himself and the man on the ground, placing his left knee on the man's back when he reached him. He then grabbed a clump of his hair and was about to land another blow when the Lakota realized it wasn't necessary. He let the head drop back to the ground and stood up.

The men behind the boulders didn't quite know what to make of what had just transpired before them. Not that they weren't relieved, but how and why did it occur? Lakota helping the US Army was a might perplexing, especially so near the Black Hills in the disputed territory. Lieutenant Carlson wasn't sure how to respond so he ordered those of his detachment to cease-fire. They did so and watched what proceeded across the trail toward the trees.

The Lakota that had just chased down the ambusher remained standing over the silent man on the ground. Off to the right, the soldiers and Brian spotted two white men on horseback emerging from the trees at full speed. They were heading northeast in the direction of the Black Hills. No Lakota followed and the two were able to make their escape.

Then all was quiet. The shooting, yelling and screaming had stopped. The Lakota that had ridden from the trees to attack the ambushers that had tried to out flank the troop were all back on their horses and heading toward the one Lakota near the trail. As they got to within twenty-five yards of the lone Indian, other Lakota on horses began coming out of the grove of trees. First came one then another and a pair followed this. In all, fourteen came from the trees and they all gathered together where the one Lakota stood over the dead ambusher.

The band of Lakota sat upon their horses facing the trail and boulders. Those behind the rocks stood looking at the Lakota; still not sure what to make of what had just happened. After another minute, with each group studying one another, one of the Lakota broke from the group and rode his horse slowly toward the boulders. After fifteen yards he stopped, raised his hand above his head for several seconds then let it drop to his side.

Lieutenant Carlson watched from the rocks, turning to Sergeant Halsey he asked, "What do you make of that?"

Halsey pushed his hat to the back of his head as he studied the scene before him. "I do believe the Indian wants to speak with us," he said

"Lieutenant I think that is the same Lakota I saved just outside Buffalo Gap two days ago," cut in Brian.

"Is that so?" responded Carlson.

"Yes, I'm sure of it," said Brian with confidence then added, "his name is Kohanna."

"You know him by name, that's got to be something in our favor," offered Marshal who was watching the Lakota intently.

"Sir, I believe it would be safe and wise to go and talk with him. We wouldn't be here now, if it weren't for their help against those that ambushed us."

"I agree," said Carlson nodding, then turning to Brian he said, "I want you to come with me. Your presence may help."

"We'll stay at the ready just in case things go sour," said Halsey putting a fresh cartridge into his carbine.

The Lieutenant and Brian laid their rifles against the boulder, climbed over the top and walked toward the waiting Lakota. As the two made their way across the trail, they noticed another Lakota had ridden out to Kohanna. The two Indians slid off their horses and moved a couple of paces to the front of them and waited for the white men. In less than a minute, Carlson and Dolan had traversed to the two Lakota standing stiffly in front of their horses. As they came closer, Brian whispered to Carlson that the Indian to their right was definitely the same one he had helped free from the miners two days ago. Carlson nodded his head. When Carlson and Dolan came within five yards of the Indians they stopped and Carlson raised his hand. Kohanna responded similarly by raising his right hand.

Carlson spoke first," Do you speak English," directing his question to Kohanna.

The Lakota next to Kohanna answered sharply," He does not. You speak to me, I to him," nodding his head toward Kohanna.

"Very well. First, we would like to thank you for your help," offered Carlson.

The Lakota turned to Kohanna and spoke to him in their native language.

Without expression the Lakota leader nodded his head then spoke without taking his eyes off either Carlson or Brian. When he was done the translator said, "He says, we saw your need and we help."

Kohanna then stepped toward Dolan and held out his hand and uttered, "Brian?"

Brian responded by stretching out his own hand and said, "I'm Brian."

They then clasped arms as they did the last time they were together and Brian asked, "Kohanna?"

The Lakota nodded again still with no expression on his face. After releasing their grip Kohanna moved back next to his partner and spoke. The other Lakota translated, "He says we are heading in direction of where sun goes down to hunt Buffalo and we see fight begin between you and other white men. We pass no interest. Let white man kill each other. Then Kohanna sees Brian in your group and wants to help as Brian helped. We in good place to attack enemy from behind."

Carlson looked at Brian then back to the two Lakota, "We again thank you for your help whatever the reason."

The translator related the last phrase to his leader. Kahonna responded with a slow nod of his head. Then he spoke as he turned to his left and waved his hand from his right to his left across the tree grove behind him.

"He says many dead white man in trees with those you see out of trees. He leave for you. We go the way of sun go down at night to hunt buffalo," related the Lakota interpreter.

" Tell Kahonna I'm glad to see he is doing well and we wish you a good hunt." said Brian

After repeating what Brian had said Kahonna spoke to Brian directly which was then spoken in English by the other Lakota.

"Kahonna thanks you. He ask Spirits to guide you, keep safe."

Kahonna then walked to his horse seized its mane and pulled himself up onto its back. His interpreter did the same and as they looked down at the two white men before them Brian tipped his hat and Carlson gave a quick salute. The two Lakota turned their horses back to the main group and Kahonna cried out to them as they passed and the group fell in behind their leader. He led them to the edge of the trees and turned in a westerly direction disappearing from sight at a leisurely gallop.

Once the Lakota were out of sight, Carlson and Dolan returned to the boulders and took stock of their situation. Lieutenant Carlson first went to where Sarah was taking care of Ridley. The private's bleeding had been stemmed and Carlson confirmed the wound was not as bad as it looked at first. Sarah had done a wonderful job bandaging the wound and making Ridley as comfortable as could be expected under the circumstances. Carlson realized it would be best to send Ridley back to Buffalo Gap, but decided the wound was not life threating and Ridley could make it the rest of the way. He rationalized that Ridley would give them an extra gun when Brian, Sarah and Jim left their group for the mining camp.

Once Carlson had verified Ridley's condition he maneuvered out onto the trail to where Private Lance Howard had been shot from his horse at the onset of the ambush. Private Howard was lying face down when Carlson came up to him. Turning him over gently the lieutenant discovered the bullet had hit him in the middle of the chest and had gone directly through the heart. Carlson called to sergeant Halsey, "Sergeant, we're over a day's ride from Fort Meade. We'll bury Dixon and Howard next to the boulders here. Take care of it, will you."

"Right away sir." answered Halsey. He then shouted orders to Marshal and Henderson to comply with the lieutenant's wishes.

The lieutenant returned to the boulders in search of Brian and Jim. Upon finding them together with Sarah he said, "I would like you two to come with me and examine the dead ambushers for any information that may tell us who they are."

"I'll do what I can lieutenant, but realize I've only been in Buffalo Gap a couple of days." said Brian adjusting his gun belt.

"I know, "acknowledged Carlson, while slapping Brian on the back of the shoulder, "but that's two more days than I've been in town so, in my book, that makes you an expert."

Giving his attention to Jim, Carlson added, "Anyway, we have Jim here, he's been a part of the town since the beginning so I'm am sure he will be able to identify any of the dead that might be from this area."

"I'll do my best," offered Jim softly.

The three then gathered their horses and rode out to the two dead ambushers just south of the boulders.

" Do either of you recognize these two?" asked Carlson.

Both men on the ground were on their backs and their faces were plainly visible.

"I have never seen these two," stated Brian.

"Nor I," said Jim

The Lieutenant then got off his horse and proceeded to go through each man's pockets looking for anything that might identify who they were. The search came up empty. Carlson remounted, "nothing from those two," he said, "maybe the others will reveal something useful."

Pulling on the reins he turned in the opposite direction toward the three dead men to the north of the boulders and kicked his horse into a swift gallop. Brian and Jim followed suit and the three covered the distance in short order. The search of the three bodies returned similar results. Nothing to disclose whom these men were or where they came from. The Lieutenant then led them into the grove to search for the dead left by the Lakota.

The three dismounted just outside the grove and entered separately to cover more ground more quickly. Brian headed for the area where the man he shot had fallen. The man was not difficult to find, he lay on his back where he had dropped. As Brian studied the man he recognized the face as one of the men that had been in the saloon the first night he had arrived in Buffalo Gap. After inspecting the body and going through his pockets, again Brian found nothing that would identify who he was or who he was working for. Getting to his feet Brian looked around him peering amongst the pines trying to find any other bodies. All he saw was Lieutenant Carlson kneeling over another body some twenty yards farther in the grove.

Working his way over to the Lieutenant Brian was taken aback slightly when he got a glimpse of the man dead on the ground. Brian recognized this man also. It was the man in the saloon that had shot the disgruntled miner and Sheriff Baker had taken to the jail.

Pushing his hat back on his head Brian said, "Well, isn't that interesting?"

"What's interesting?" asked the lieutenant as he continued his examination of the dead man.

"I know this guy, well, I 've seen him before anyway," said Brian as he kneeled next to the lieutenant.

"Oh yeah? Who is he?"

Clearing his throat Brian explained, " The first night in town while the sheriff and I were having dinner at the saloon there was an altercation between this man and a miner that ended in this man shooting and killing the miner. He was arrested by the sheriff and escorted to jail."

Rifling through the dead man's vest pockets Carlson said, "Obviously the sheriff decided he wasn't guilty."

"Yes, I was thinking the same thing," responded Brian slowly with a furrowed brow.

"Curious, first the incident in the saloon dealing with the miners, then he shows up here in an ambush on a gold shipment from the mines, and, you put that together with the other body back there," pointed Brian in the direction of the man he had searched, "I saw that man in the saloon the night this man killed the miner. It would seem there is more involved here than just a coincidence."

Finding nothing of use in his search, Carlson stood up and walked to the other dead bodies lying within the grove. Carlson and Brian examined the last four bodies without turning up anymore-useful information. They returned to their horses mounted and rode back to the rest of the detachment at the boulders. Just as they crossed the trail, private Marshal met them and said," Sir, we have Dixon and Howard buried and the wagon is ready to go."

"Good work private. Take Ridley, Henderson and Halsey with you and gather all the weapons from the ambushers. Put them in the wagon. When that's done we'll head out for the fort."

Before Marshal could respond a voice behind Marshal cut in, "Lieutenant we can't leave just yet. What about the bodies of the ambushers, you can't just abandon them out in the open. They need to be buried as well."

All heads turned in the direction of Sarah who was standing behind Marshal. Carlson stared at Sarah then said, "Miss Schuler, I understand you mean well but we don't have the time and with a wounded man we need to get to Fort Meade as soon as possible."

Sarah took two steps toward the lieutenant, put her hands on her hips and said, “For a situation like this, one makes the time, and as far as private Ridley, his wound is not serious and we have bandaged him well enough that a slight delay will not endanger him in the slightest."

"Those ambushers don't deserve to be buried, they jumped us

without warning and killed Dixon and Howard," snapped Marshal.

"There is no reason for men to be left to the animals to be dismembered and eaten if it can be prevented," said Sarah to Marshal then speaking to the entire group she added, "It's the right thing to do. If we don't bury them, we are no better than those that attacked us. Remember there were two that got away and they will be telling their version of the incident. How will it look for you and your men if we don't bury the dead?"

No one spoke. They all pondered what Sarah had just said. After a short moment Carlson broke the silence choosing his words carefully, "I don't know about your religious reasoning for burying these dead men, but I do see it may be a good move for our relationship with the people in this area since the recent treaty with the Lakota along with this recent discovery of gold in the area, the US army has been put in difficult situation to please both sides. Maybe it is best to bury these men to smooth over the conflict of the past six months."

Giving his attention to Sergeant Halsey, Carlson asked, " Sergeant how is Ridley's condition?"

"Well sir, to be honest, Miss Schuler has done a fine job on his wound and it is as she says. He can travel."

"But sir!" exclaimed Marshal, you aren't seriously considering---"

"That will be enough private!" commanded Carlson firmly, "if Sergeant Halsey says Ridley can travel, then we'll take the time to bury the dead."

"Yes sir, "replied Marshal with a displeased look on his face.

Seeing what had just transpired Brian was coming to the realization that Sarah was different than all the women that he had previously known. She was outspoken, bold, compassionate, and with all that she was easy on the eyes. He wanted to get to know her better.

Chapter 8

The stream gurgled and splashed as it rushed down toward the valley below. Brian, Jim, and Sarah had been traveling along the stream for the past hour carefully working their way along the trail over rocks and roots that had been exposed from the continuous use by travelers to and from the mines. Though their progress had been slow, the trio would reach the mining area well before dark.

Adjusting her bottom in the saddle again, Sarah said, "Mr. Middlebrook, how much longer before we reach the mines?"

Without looking back Middlebrook squawked, "At the most, another fifteen minutes."

"Thank goodness. Not that I'm complaining, but my back end has endured all the riding it can handle for a day," said Sarah with relief.

"You're doing quite well under the circumstances, Miss Schuler," piped in Brian.

"Thank you Mr. Dolan," replied Sarah allowing a small smile to cross her lips. "But please, call me Sarah."

"Yes ma'am, Sarah it is," said Brian.

"And you, may I address you as Brian?" asked Sarah.

"That would be fine," answered Brian.

Just then the trio came upon a smaller stream. It cut directly across their path and approximately five yards from where the smaller stream flowed into the main stream several large boulders along with a log some three feet in diameter created a small dam. This formed a large pool on the upper side which forced the trail to turn sharply to the right and head up a small tributary about twenty yards before continuing on the other side. Jim steered his horse to the right and followed the trail to where it entered the stream. Without hesitation he prodded his horse to wade through to the opposite bank. Sarah and Brian followed, their horses splashing through the shallow portion of the stream.

Once on the other side, the trail cut back and then continued along the bank of the larger stream. As Sarah's horse turned right to follow the lead horse along the bank, she said to no one in particular, "This is such beautiful country. I look around and see the trees, wildlife, and streams and I wonder how people can't believe there is a God."

After a short pause Jim spoke, "God, why does there have to be a God involved? Mother Nature can take care of herself quite nicely."

"You believe that the complexity of life and the beauty of these surrounding hills is all do to chance?" exclaimed Sarah.

"I wouldn't say it was by chance, Miss Schuler. After reading Darwin's book, I would say it was through the process he described as evolution, or more specifically, his theory of Natural Selection."

"Evolution," responded Sarah with a chuckle. "That is the new popular theory on how man came to be."

"It makes sense," retorted Jim.

"I will admit that looking at it on the surface one can be lulled into believing its premise, but if you look at it more closely you realize most of what his theory speaks of is just speculation. There are so many major gaps that cannot be explained or even trusted," expounded Sarah.

"Such as?" inquired Brian.

"For one thing, to my knowledge the changing of one species into another has never been directly observed. Only speculation theorizes that that has occurred," said Sarah.

"True, the process takes too long for man to see it directly, but we have all the fossils as evidence." retorted Jim.

"Exactly, there are the fossils, but again speculation is at work. Scientist don't have any direct proof by looking at the skeletal remains of a fossil that it is a direct ancestor of another fossil that is determined to be younger in age. They are just assuming there is a connection," stated Sarah.

"If my memory serves me correctly didn't Darwin see evidence of the change of species on the islands off the coast of Ecuador?" asked Jim sharply.

"He was comparing the characteristics of those animals found on the islands and those found on the mainland of South America. There were slight differences in the two, but the differences were only in their characteristics. The finches on the mainland are still finches on the islands.

They hadn't changed into lizards for example," replied Sarah.

"Okay then, let's look at your belief in God. What proof or evidence is there that this is the correct origin of man?" asked Brian.

Sarah didn't answer immediately. She looked straight ahead her eyes fixed upon the horse plodding along the trail in front of her. Brian could tell she was in deep thought about the question he had just given her. After a minute she broke her stare from the horse in front and said," For my first evidence I go back to the question I asked a few moments ago." Gesturing with her hand Sarah drew the attention of the other two to all that was about them. "Look around you. The beauty you see of the stream, the forest, the wildlife and the mountains speaks for itself. Only a divine power could create such loveliness. All this by chance, I don't think so."

"Pretty flimsy evidence if you ask me," snorted Jim. "You're just speculating yourself."

"Speculating? In the Bible the first chapter of Romans tells us that through the creation of the world, God's attributes and His eternal power have been clearly seen and understood. No one is without excuse to the knowledge of God."

"Hold on miss. Who says the Bible is the authority of all things?" shot back Jim.

"For me it is. I believe in the word of God," replied Sarah.

"Debating the truth of the Bible is not going to accomplish anything either way at this time. I suggest we find out Sarah's second piece of evidence for God being the creator of man," offered Brian.

"Fine, we can discuss the Bible later," said Jim reluctantly.

"The second evidence somewhat piggybacks the first. If you look at the complexity of life, how can you come to any other conclusion but that there is a God at work." said Sarah.

"Isn't that what evolution is all about? Animals going from simple to more complex over a long period of time," stated Jim haughtily.

"Yes, in its simplest form, but all those changes occurred by chance. How could that result in the miracles of life we see today? Take the wonder of an unborn child during pregnancy. I don't see how an amoeba from long ago could by chance change into the complex humans we are today, especially when seeing the growth of the baby through the nine months before birth." countered Sarah.

Pulling on the reins, Jim stopped his horse and maneuvered him to the left then said to Sarah, "It would seem your proof, again, is pretty weak, in fact it is no solid proof at all just an assumption."

"It is all the proof one needs if you examine the world around us and study God's word," said Sarah.

"I would rather put my faith in what the scientist have to say on the matter,' retorted Jim.

"That's the crux of the matter," exclaimed Sarah rising off her saddle, "evolutionary theory is based on faith just like the Bible. As I said before, there is no direct scientific proof that animals have changed from one species into another."

Jim did not respond, but instead jabbed his horse with his heels and moved up the trail at a speed slightly faster than a walk. Sarah and Brian followed. After a few minutes Jim slowed his pace to a comfortable stroll, and Sarah and Brian settled in behind once again plodding their way toward the mines in silence. This continued for another quarter of a mile before Brian broke the stillness by speaking to Sarah.

"I was thinking about what you two were discussing down the trail, it seems, I need to do some reading."

"Reading of what?" asked Sarah.

"To get a better grasp on the debate you two were having, I think I need to get a hold of Darwin's book along with a copy of the Bible."

"Have you read the Bible Brian?"

"I have to admit, I never have." said Brian

"I don't know about getting a copy of Darwin's book out here in the Black Hills, but you certainly can borrow my copy of the Bible anytime. That is if you are truly interested in reading it."

"You've pricked my interest in this God of yours, and the Bible seems a good way to find out who he is and what he is about, " said Brian with sincerity.

"There is no better place to do so," concurred Sarah as she reached back and tapped the saddlebag lying across her horse's backbone, "I carry a small Bible with me whenever I travel and the next free moment I'll get it out for you."

"Thanks. Much appreciated," said Brian.

Up front Jim called over his shoulder, "We're getting close."

On either side of the stream the group saw large piles of earth in front of holes dug into the hill. They were abandoned mines that had been left unworked for quite some time. The excavated soil was not new and there was very little equipment about. There was not a person to be seen.

"These were the first claims to be dug when prospectors came into the area and as you can see their production of gold was pretty slim," pointed out Jim. "It wasn't until a little further upstream that gold of any quantity was obtained. That was what really got this region noticed."

Riding past these initial claims, Brian tried to imagine the thoughts of the men that came hoping to find their riches, only to discover their attempts were fruitless. He wondered if they persevered and continued their search further upstream or did they give up and return to wherever they had come from. How would have he reacted? He hoped he would be one that persisted beyond one quick attempt before giving up. Not because of the gold alone and its riches but because it was his nature to work hard and finish what he started. At times that was easier said than done he had to admit.

As they continued along the stream more and more abandoned holes showed themselves. It looked like some large burrowing animal had worked its way up the gully digging a new hole after vacating the previous one. Suddenly the gorge the stream traveled opened up into a wide basin that contained gradual slopes on each side of the stream. Within this basin was located the main mining operation of the area. Scattered throughout the basin were small wooden buildings in amongst numerous white canvas tents.

Further up the basin where the walls of the canyon narrowed, were wooden sluices that reached from the stream up toward the canyon walls. Even from a distance Brian and Sarah saw the busy activity of human labor along the wooden channels as the men worked diligently to extract the gold from the earth. On the right just as the basin began to narrow was located Langston's operation. Not only could they see there were more men working along the sluice, it was the only claim with permanent wooden structures at the upper end of the mine. The three worked their way up the stream as Sarah and Brian studied all that was before them with keen interest.

"The one furthest up this bowl is where we're headed," said Middlebrook as they neared the first claim on their side of the river.

"Quite primitive, the living conditions that is," insisted Sarah.

"That's a mining camp for you," stated Middlebrook guiding his horse to the right in order to maneuver around the first sluice.

The men working the claim briefly looked up from their labor as the three passed along the man-made channel toward the oversize barrel that held the water to rinse the soil from the precious metal. There were no smiles, no pleasant greetings, only grim faces with blank stares. Then, they were back to work toiling the claim as if the riders had never passed.

Jim guided Sarah and Brian around the sluice and then worked his way directly toward a cluster of three buildings. The building furthest up the slope was the largest of the three being twice the size of the other two. It faced the stream and was built on a slight plateau that ran parallel to the stream. It had a single window placed in the middle of the wall facing the riders. The other two structures were situated one after the other about ten yards to the south. Neither of these structures had windows.

As the three came near the buildings Brian noticed that the trees growing on their side of the stream had been removed. Looking farther up the ridge behind the structures Brian also observed the number of trees increased, practically covering the entire ridge near the top. Scanning the ridge on the opposite side of the stream, he noted a similar situation.

Jim brought his horse to a stop directly in front of the largest structure and dismounted. He loosely tied the reins to one of the hitching post and motioned for Sarah and Brian to do the same. Once dismounted, the two followed Jim up to the front of the building. Sarah was pleased to be off the horse and on her own two feet again. It had been a long day from Buffalo Gap.

Lifting up the latch Jim pushed the door open and stepped inside. Upon reaching the doorway Brian stepped to the side and gestured for Sarah to enter next. Sarah smiled and walked into the structure. Brian followed and took in the contents of the well-lit room.

Scanning the room Brian saw a small simple table and chair off to his left. To the right of the table was a three drawer file cabinet and at the back of the room against the wall was a small plain wooden bed with a couple of blankets and a pillow. To the right was a long table with three chairs on each side.

"Welcome to the Buffalo Mining Company's on site office and dining hall," said Jim directly to Brian, "and your new place of residence.

"Simple, but looks to be quite adequate." Brian assured him.

"It has served its purpose so far," agreed Jim, "eventually, this will be your place of residence, but for now you and I will bunk together in the far structure. Miss Schuler will be using this building while she is here. It is by far the roomiest and will allow for the most privacy."

"I agree with Mr. Dolan," concurred Sarah looking the room over," it will be quite comfortable. Thank you Mr. Middlebrook."

"Good. Glad to hear it." said Jim cheerfully. He then turned his attention to the table and chair that served as the office for the building.

"This is where you will be taking care of the paper work."

Suddenly there was an enormous explosion from outside the building. All three within the office froze. Within an instant, Brian recovered, and dashed to the door. Peering through the doorway, he studied the outside for a moment then stepped outside. Sarah and Jim quickly followed.

Chapter 9

Once outside, Brian quickly saw the source of the explosion. Across the stream about a hundred yards down from the Mining Company office, dust and smoke were rising from the entrance of a tunnel dug into the ridge. Men were running toward the tunnel entrance from other claims.

From behind Brian Jim cried, " I'm going to grab some medical supplies from the storage shack! Looks like a cave in."

Jim raced to the far shack, darted inside, and in less than a minute came out holding several items in his hands. He ran back toward the main office building and, as he passed by Brian and Sarah, he shouted," follow me!"

Brian and Sarah could see that Jim was heading for a make shift bridge just up the stream from where they were. The two fell in behind Middlebrook and they made their way across the narrow bridge and down the stream to the entrance of the mine. When they reached the mine, there were several men already frantically removing debris from the opening. Along with shoveling dirt and rock, they were pulling broken timber from the pile that had accumulated in front of the entrance. A man with large arms and a barrel chest appeared to be in charge. While he was pulling supporting beams half buried in the dirt he said in a booming voice, "Bill! Shovel at the top left. Max you work on the lower middle area just above this beam!"

The two men responded sharply and attacked the two spots with their shovels. Other men were working on the sides of the entrance clearing away as much of the dirt as possible. By now a crowd had gathered around the mine entrance watching those that were in the process of unblocking the entrance. Middlebrook shouted to no one in particular, "How many are trapped inside?"

While yanking on a timber the barrel-chested man grunted, "Two---

Jethro and Sonny."

"How far in were they?" asked Middlebrook.

A tall slender man in a faded red shirt working the left side of the opening with a shovel said, "not sure exactly, I had just gone down to the stream to get water when she caved in."

Middlebrook looked the crowd over then shouted, "Any one see what happened?"

The throng of miners talked amongst themselves but no one admitted to seeing what had occurred when the shaft collapsed. A small stout man wearing jeans with an un-tucked dirty gray shirt said to Middlebrook, "That was definitely an explosion that caused the mine to cave in!"

Another miner overhearing him piped, "Ya, we seem to be having our share of accidents lately."

"I agree," said a third, "that's the fourth one in a week."

"Hold on!" barked Middlebrook, "let's not get crazy here. We need to concentrate on getting Jethro and Sonny out. We can discuss these accidents later."

The two men didn't respond, they just turned their attention back to those working to free the two trapped miners. Brian on the other hand kept his focus upon Middlebrook. He had heard the comments of the two miners and his interest in the operation of this mining camp was going to go beyond the job description Langston had given him back in Buffalo Gap. Something was not quite right and hadn't been since his first night in the saloon when the miner was shot. Brian was curious to find out what was going on. He was sure the Buffalo Mining Company was involved, but in what way he did not know.

"Here's a hand!" cried the slender man in the faded red shirt.

"Use your hands to dig!" boomed the barrel-chested man; "We don't want to injure him with the shovels."

The slender man with the faded red shirt threw down his shovel and dropped to his hands and knees and started digging around the exposed hand. Two other men joined in and they quickly uncovered the buried man to his shoulder. Once to the shoulder they took a little more care removing the dirt and rock. Shortly they had his head visible and the slender man with the faded red shirt yelled," It's Sonny!"

"Careful now, careful" instructed the barrel-chested man, while he gently took hold of Sonny's head so the others could continue to remove dirt from around his body. After clearing the dirt down to his waist they were able to grasp Sonny under his arms and pull him free. The barrel-chested man and the man with the faded red shirt carried him ten yards from the pile of dirt and gently laid him down. Middlebrook immediately came to Sonny's side and placed his ear down on the man's chest. After a several seconds Middlebrook stated, "He's alive."

A roar went up from the crowd of miners and those continuing to dig for Jethro intensified their efforts. Middlebrook then briefly examined Sonny, looking for any serious lacerations or broken bones. He found none.

"There seems to be nothing seriously wrong with him," said Middlebrook leaning back from the injured man, "He does have a good size bump on the top of his head, most likely from a timber falling when the tunnel collapsed."

"Is there anything I can do to help?" asked Sarah from just behind Middlebrook's left shoulder.

Lifting his face towards Sarah, Middlebrook replied, "Thanks, but I think for the moment we'll just let him rest and see if he comes to shortly."

"Please, let me know if there is anything I can do," insisted Sarah with concern.

"Yes ma'am, I will," said Middlebrook.

Except for Middlebrook, all the attention returned to the work being done to dig out the other miner. The barrel-chested man had gone back to the entrance of the mine and was giving instructions once again. The opening had been cleared several yards but no sign of Jethro had been revealed.

"Dig faster!" bellowed the barrel-chested man, "We don't know how much air he has buried under all that dirt. Every minute counts."

The digging increased. After several minutes the rescuers finally broke through the dirt, rocks and timbers into the shaft. Once a large enough hole was cleared the barrel-chested man stepped to the hole and stuck his head into the opening.

After a moment he pulled his head from the hole and said," It's too dark. I can't see anything. We need to make the hole larger."

Stepping back from the hole he motioned for those with shovels to increase the size of the cavity. Then turning to the man with the faded red shirt he ordered, "Bart, get a lantern and bring it here!"

Bart darted to the next mine upstream. While he was gone other miners moved to the collapsed entrance and worked on enlarging the opening into the mineshaft. When Bart returned, the hole was the width of a medium size man's waist. The barrel-chested man took the lantern from Bart and gestured for the men digging to move from the hole. With two hands he cautiously guided the bottom of the lantern through the hole. Moving the lantern into the mineshaft as far as his shoulder he then leaned his face up against the opening.

"What do you see Jack? " asked Bart anxiously.

"Nothing yet," snarled Jack, "give me chance will ya."

"Okay, Ya, sure," responded Bart sheepishly.

It seemed like an eternity until Jack cried out, "I see him!"

"Is he alive?" inquired Bart.

"Can't tell yet," said Jack lifting his head from the hole and pulling the lantern out, "He's just beyond all this debris. He's face down with a large beam across his back."

Moving back from the pile he added, "Go ahead and get that hole opened enough so we can reach him."

In another five minutes the blocked shaft had been cleared enough that Jack was able to crawl into the tunnel. Sliding down on his belly to the floor of the tunnel, Jack was able to reach Jethro without disturbing the pile of debris. Jack swung himself around so that he was sitting next to the trapped man's upper body. He touched the man's shoulder and shook it gently. There was no response. Jack then got on his knees and tried lifting the beam off of Jethro but he discovered quickly that his position didn't allow the leverage necessary. Getting to his feet Jack shifted to the end of the beam where he could get a grip underneath it. Squatting as low as he could he grasped the beam and lifted with all his strength. Slowly the beam came up off the trapped man. When Jack had it a couple of inches above the man's back, he shuffled to his left. Strain showing clearly on his face, Jack let the beam drop to the floor just past Jethro's feet.

Jack bent over and placed his hands on his knees and relaxed for a moment. He then returned to Jethro and lightly turned him onto his back. Kneeling next to him he checked for breathing by placing his ear on Jethro's chest. Nothing. Leaning back on his knees he yelled, "Bart get in here and help me get Jethro out!"

"Be right there," said Bart.

The light from the lantern disappeared and then the shaft went dark as

Bart squirmed through the opening into the tunnel. Sliding down the pile just as Jack had, Bart came to the bottom of the pile at the feet of Jack.

"I don't know if he's alive or not. We'll assume he is. You take his feet and I'll grab him under the shoulders," said Jack placing himself above Jethro's head.

Bart moved to the unconscious man's feet and clutched his ankles. The two men struggled up the slope of the pile of dirt to the opening. Being as gentle as they could it was not easy getting the body up the slope. The two men ended up having to pull and push the body on their knees to the gap leading to the outside. Once they reached the opening, those outside seized Jethro by the shoulders and dragged him through.

Outside Jethro was carried over to where Sonny was lying and placed carefully on his back. Jim checked for life the same way he had done for Sonny by placing an ear on Jethro's chest and felt for breathing. After a moment Jim moved his head closer to the man's throat and listened again. Another moment went by and again he moved his head over Jethro's left lung and listened for a third time. By this time, all the miners had crowded around waiting to hear if Jethro was alive or not. Middlebrook raised his head slowly shaking it back forth then said, "No good. He's dead."

"What rotten luck," said a miner in the back of the crowd, "They were just beginning to bring out a good amount of gold from this claim."

A miner next to Brian said under his breath with a disgusted tone, "Rotten luck---the way things are going, when a claim begins to produce, something bad happens. Luck, I'm not so sure."

"Ain't that the truth," whispered another.

A third miner said, "I'm wondering if it's worth hitting it big?"

The first miner that had spoken growled, "Just watch your backs boys." He then turned and walked away from the crowd.

Brian wanted to hear more from this miner. He took his leave from the group and swiftly caught up with the miner. As Brian came alongside, the miner gave Brian a look but said nothing and kept heading toward the next mine.

"Excuse me," said Brian keeping step with the miner, "I couldn't help over hear what you said back there."

"So what!" snapped the miner.

"I'm the new mine foreman for the Buffalo Gap Company and I 'm interested in what you meant by luck not being the driving force behind the recent accidents."

"Why would I tell you anything?" snarled the miner.

"I was hired to make sure things run smoothly for the Buffalo Gap Company and all information leading to the safety of those working for the company would help."

"Hey, what can I tell you?" said the miner stopping next to the sluice that was apparently part of his claim. Facing Brian he continued, "Are these accidents, I don't know for sure, it's just that the last four or five accidents have happened in a very short time. In each case the claim just started to give a good return. Coincidence? The first two, maybe. But this many, this quickly? Let's just say I have my doubts."

"I must admit it does sound a bit odd," said Brian puzzled, "You say this has only been the last week or two, these accidents?

The miner rubbed the side of his face while looking over Brian's right shoulder pondering what Brian had just asked. After several seconds he shook his finger slowly in front of his face and said, "Yep, as I think back, up until a couple of weeks ago things were pretty normal. Of course there were the usual accidents that occur, but these were far and few between."

"I'll check into these accidents. Maybe we can find out what's going on." said Brian.

"That would be much appreciated," said the miner gratefully. "As it is, there are more and more of us getting a bit spooked about working our claims."

"I'll let you know if I find out anything. By the way my name is Brian Dolan," said Brian offering his hand.

The miner took it and said, "My name is Luke Adams. My friends call me Lefty."

"It's good to make your acquaintance. I hope in the near future to earn the right to call you Lefty," responded Brian.

Brian then left Luke to his mine and returned to the mine that had collapsed with more questions circling in his head. What had he gotten himself into by taking this job?

Chapter 10

The sun was just creeping above the ridge taking away the chill of the morning. Brian was thankful for warmth as it bathed his body. Scooping cold water from the bucket and splashing his face, he found the impact of the chilling liquid broke his night's stupor. His eyes fluttered wide as he gasped from the cold. Reaching into the bucket again he braced himself for the shock of the chilly water, and then dowsed another scoop into his face and rinsed away any sleep that remained.

Taking the towel lying on the log next to the bucket, Brian dried his face and then surveyed the camp before him. This being the fourth day since his arrival, Brian had fallen into a routine while learning the mining camp's daily set of tasks. Thinking back to that first day, he was pleased at how far he had come in his knowledge of the camp's operation. Particularly in light of how that first day had begun, with the cave in, the death of one miner and the serious injury of another. Not the way he wanted his new job to begin. But in short order, he was able to deal with it and get to the job at hand. The only frustration that lingered for Brian from the accident was in not being able to make any headway on finding the reason for the cave in. Of course, everyone knew it was from an explosion but what caused the explosion? Was it an accident or intentional, as some miners believed. None of Brian's questions had as yet been answered.

The two witnesses that could shed some light as to what truly happened were unable to tell their story. Jethro was dead and Sonny, who survived with a head injury, had no recollection of the explosion, or even the day leading up to the accident. Brian had been unable to piece together any hard evidence to show whether the cave in was deliberate or not. Though, speaking with the miners, several suspected some kind of foul play.

As he finished drying his face, he saw Sarah coming down the slope from the main office. Even this early in the morning as he watched her approach he noticed her unassuming beauty. Brian figured this lady could hold her own in whatever situation she found herself. She had accustomed herself with relative ease out here in the primitive wilds of a mining camp and he was sure that she could rub elbows with the high society of New York City with the same ease.

She was not one to sit back, a passive spectator. First, when Sonny needed care after the accident, Sarah, without hesitation, stepped into the role of caregiver. Then, as Sonny regained consciousness and his health improved this lady from Pennsylvania steered her attention to the mines. She asked questions about their operation and helped with the physical work from time to time where needed. Yet, she did all this without being forward or obnoxious.

When Sarah reached the log Brian was using to hold his wash bucket he said with a pleasant voice, "Good morning Miss Schuler, and how are you this fine morning?"

"Remember, it's Sarah," said Sarah with a playful reprimand in her tone.

"Yes ma'am---I mean, Sarah," replied Brian.

"I am doing well though I could freshen up a bit," said Sarah pointing to the bucket on the log, “is that fresh water?"

"Yes, I just filled it not 3 minutes ago."

"May I use some, " asked Sarah placing her hands together in front of her face, "I must be a sight."

"You look fine," replied Brian stepping from the log and pointing to the bucket, "and by all means, it's all yours."

Stepping to the bucket Sarah reached in with both hands and repeated the gesture Brian had performed a minute before. Dipping her hands into the bucket she exclaimed, "Oh that's cold!"

Hesitating a moment she took a deep breath then threw the cold water onto her face. She reacted with a gasp, but quickly rubbed her face with her hands and leaned forward to allow the excess water to drip from her face without letting it get on her clothing.

"Here," said Brian grabbing Sarah's left wrist and guiding her hand to the cloth he had used to dry his face. The grasp upon her wrist was firm but gentle, something she had not expected from a man that had spent most of his adult life traveling and working jobs far from the civilized world.

Surprisingly it was not unpleasant. Touching the cloth he held for her brought her mind swiftly back to the water on her face and she quickly dried it. Handing the cloth back to Brian she said, "Thank you, for the water and the towel."

"My pleasure." stated Brian dropping the cloth onto the rim of the bucket. "So what are your impressions of mining camp life?"

Not answering directly Sarah moved to the log and sat down, then shifting her head toward Brian she said," When I first decided to come out and visit Uncle Virgil all I knew of mining were stories I had read in the newspaper. Those stories focused on the gold being taken easily from the ground. In reality, the work is hard and the return for the most part is minimal. I definitely have come to appreciate the difficulties the men in this camp have to face."

"Difficulties. Interesting word you've chosen," said Brian sitting down next to Sarah. "It is true that all camps have their difficulties, and challenges, but this camp seems to attract them like no other."

"What are you saying?" inquired Sarah

"What I'm saying is this camp has had more than its share of misfortune," responded Brian. "True it could all be coincidental, but after the cave in our first day here and then talking with the miners these past few days, I have a suspicion that there is more behind this than just bad luck."

"You mean to say these accidents are deliberate?" asked Sarah.

"Again, I have no hard evidence to that fact, but yes, I am beginning to believe there is someone behind all the accidents," said Brian shifting his body so that he was facing Sarah.

"But why would anyone do such a thing?" asked Sarah with furrowed brow.

"Good question," responded Brian. "But think back to the ambush we ran into on the way up here. I'm sure there a connection between that and what has been happening."

Sitting next to Sarah with the morning sun fully upon her face, Brian was again struck by her simple beauty. He realized he enjoyed their time together, alone.

"What are you going to do now?" inquired Sarah.

"Just continue to keep my eyes and ears open. Maybe something will shed some light on all this."

"I can give you a couple of extra eyes and ears," offered Sarah.

"I thank you but I don't want to put you in harm's way," said Brian placing a hand on Sarah's shoulder. "We don't know who we're dealing with. If someone is behind all this, it is obvious that killing is not beyond their conscience."

Sarah smiled and said, "I appreciate your concern, but two working together will give a better chance of finding out if there is anything to this," then with a straight face, " I assure you I will be careful."

"I'm not going to argue with you," responded Brian. "You're a big girl and you can make your own decisions. Your help is welcomed, but as you said, let us both be careful."

Brian stood up and seized the water bucket as Sarah raised herself from the log. Facing each other, Brian stated, "With Middlebrook going back to Buffalo Gap yesterday you and I are the only ones directly connected to the Buffalo Mining Company. Of course there are the miners working your uncle's claim but my guess is they wouldn't have any direct knowledge of the mines operation. Let's keep any information to ourselves until we get a grasp on what is happening, if anything."

"Agreed." said Sarah.

The two then walked up the slope toward the office building.

"Later this morning I'm going to be inspecting one of your uncle's claims, care to join me?" asked Brian.

"I would be glad to," replied Sarah with a show of excitement in her voice. "Will you be inspecting inside the mine?"

"Yes, I will," stated Brian.

"Good. I've been wanting to see the inside of a mine."

"I hope it meets your expectations. Some would say it is just a hole in the ground."

"Oh I don't think I will be disappointed," said Sarah turning her head toward Brian, "I find this all fascinating."

"Okay then, I'll meet you here at the office at 9:00 and we'll go down together."

"9:00 it is," confirmed Sarah with a smile, "I look forward to it."

Brian watched Sarah disappear into the office, then walked to the building that had lodged him since coming to the mining camp. It was simple, just one room housing two beds along with one small table and chair. Though not luxurious, it met his needs adequately. He remembered the many times he'd lodged in conditions much worse than this clean and dry structure. Add the fact that Middlebrook had returned to Buffalo Gap, Brian enjoyed the extra space and added peacefulness. Finally, with Middlebrook gone, Brian was able to go about his business without the watchful eyes of someone from the Mining Company. He was free to go where he wanted to and do what he thought was best.

After dressing and then wrapping his six-gun around his waist Brian snatched his hat off the chair next to the table and stepped outside. Surveying the camp for a second he placed his hat on his head and pulled it down tightly. He saw his horse tethered and ambling over to the animal, he gathered the reins and lifted himself into the saddle. It was still early in the morning but Brian could see several men along the river and next to the sluices preparing for another day of mining. The foreman of the Buffalo Company gently pulled on the reins, guiding his horse up stream away from the activity of the camp. He wanted to spend some time in the canyon above the basin studying the area.

Brian kept away from the stream as he rode up the gentle slope of the basin. There were two mining claims between his office and where the stream entered the basin from the canyon. By keeping his distance, it was much easier to negotiate past these two mines.

Coming to the first claim, Brian observed no activity along the sluice, in the mine or even at the tent that was pitched some twenty yards from the entrance of the mine. He presumed this outfit chose sleep over gold this particular morning. Can't blame them, thought Brian. Sluice mining is grueling work and day after day, it wears a man down. Taking his time Brian led his horse around the holding tank at the top of the sluice, trying to be as quiet as possible. If it was sleep they wanted, Brian was going do his best to allow them that luxury.

The next claim, seventy yards up the stream, was an extreme opposite of the one he had just ridden through. Activity abounded with several men already working the claim. As he came closer Brian saw one man hunched over the sluice sifting the rocks and dirt as the water flowed down the man-made canal. Off to the right were two other men; the first was just coming from the entrance to the mine struggling with a large burlap sack slung over his shoulder. The second was at the holding tank waiting, it seemed to Brian, for instructions to open the gate that would permit more water to travel down the sluice.

The man with the burlap sack stopped and dropped the load he was carry to the ground. Seeing Brian approaching he called out, "Early start eh Mr. Dolan."

"Not as early as you and your brothers from the looks of it," called back Brian

" True we've been at it since first morning's light," said the man reaching into his back pocket. Pulling out a dirty red scarf, he mopped his forehead and added, "it's already starting to warm up, even this early."

"Are you here to give us a hand?" yelled the man at the holding tank with a laugh.

"I wish I could Bill," replied Brian with smile, "but I want to explore the canyon up above your claim before my commitment at the McMahon's mine later this morning."

"How convenient," shot back Bill sarcastically.

By this time the third brother at the sluice had turned from his work and directed his attention to the conversation. He then joined by asking with a serious tone, "Why are you exploring the canyon?"

Brian shifted his view to the third brother and said, "As the new Forman of the Buffalo Mining Company I want to know all about this operation, even where the gold first came from."

"Come on Justin, don't be so suspicious," cried Bill from above, "let the man do his job!"

"Just curious, that's all," shot back Justin.

"You have to excuse our brother's attitude. All these accidents---have us on our guard," said the miner with the burlap sack.

"Quite all right," stated Brian with the sweep of his hand, "I don't blame you and I hope to learn something that may help eliminate those concerns."

"More power to ya!" boomed Bill.

"Have a nice ride Mr. Dolan," grunted the man next to Brian while throwing the sack over his shoulder.

"Thanks and good luck to you today," responded Brian nudging his horse forward.

The three brothers then went about their business as though Brian wasn't there. Hunting for gold was a hard and tedious affair driven by the prospect of hitting it rich. A distraction of a simple greeting was not enough to keep serious miners from their pursuit of the precious metal.

Once past the brothers' claim, Brian had no more diversions from miners or mines to slow his progress up the basin to the canyon. It was not far to the cut in the ridge where the stream flowed into the lower country. He guided his horse at a leisurely pace taking in the beauty of the stream as it tumbled down into the valley. The gap he was traveling narrowed as he approached the entrance to the canyon.

As he came near the entrance he noticed the canyon was much wider than he had anticipated when he had first observed it from the camp. On either side of the stream the slope of the canyon extended at a gentle angle to the rim of the canyon. Brian was surprised to see a good growth of Ponderosa Pine all through the canyon. Pausing for a moment, he studied the stream as it cut its way down the middle of the ravine. As he looked higher up the canyon he saw that the stream splashed over rocks and boulders that had long ago fallen from the edges of the canyon.

Brian's eyes then fell upon what looked to be a trail that cut through the pines. Whether it was an animal trail or one used by the Lakota he could not tell. Tapping his horse with the heel of his boots, Brian directed the animal onto the trail. As he entered the stand of trees, the scent of the pines became stronger. He took a slow deep breath to enjoy the fragrance to its fullest. He thought to himself, *if I was to ever settle down in one place it would be hard to beat a place in or near a forest full of pines.*

Suddenly his attention was drawn to a sound about thirty yards up the canyon. Swinging his eyes swiftly to the source, he placed his hand on the handle of his pistol. Looking up the slope all that met his eyes were scattered trees and the sparse undergrowth among them. He saw nothing out of the ordinary and everything was still. Bringing his horse to a stop, he listened intently. He moved his gaze slowly from right to left peering up the slope and trying to make out anything that might have caused the sound. All was as it should be, no sound, no movement, nothing at all.

Whatever it was, was well hidden or was no longer in the vicinity. Brian waited another minute studying the slope carefully to make sure there was nothing in amongst the trees. Still only silence met his ears. With senses more alert, Brian urged his horse to continue up the trail. Taking it slow and rotating his head from left to right he investigated the stream, trail, and forest as he moved his way up the canyon. After ten minutes of riding nothing else unusual occurred and Brian discovered the canyon held a typical stream bordered on both sides with a standard forest of pines.

Nothing revealed itself that would raise any suspicions on the accidents occurring within the mines down in the basin. As he turned his horse back down the trail the disturbance did not settle well in his mind. It could be nothing, just a branch falling, but again with all the accidents in the mines, maybe it was more, maybe someone was watching him.

Chapter 11

As the sun rose above the eastern ridge, Brian could tell summer was just around the corner. He could feel its warmth even at this hour of the morning. His ride back from the canyon had been uneventful. Now as he looked up toward the office, he saw Sarah sitting on the step waiting to join him to inspect the McMahon mine. The mining company foreman turned his horse in the direction of the office and waved. Sarah stood up and waved back.

Upon reaching the office building Brian said, "Sorry if I'm a bit late. My time up in the canyon took longer than I had anticipated."

"That's alright Brian. I've not been waiting that long," responded Sarah smiling.

"Still want to check out the McMahon mine?" asked Brian

"Certainly!" stated Sarah stepping down from the office porch, "lead on."

"Let me tether my horse then we can walk down together," said Brian.

Tugging on the reins Brian led his horse to the hitching post in front of his lodging. He dismounted and secured the reins onto the ring hanging from the post. Returning to Sarah he held out his arm. Sarah grasped it, and the two of them headed down along the stream to the McMahon mine.

The mine was the second one located downstream from the Buffalo Mining Company on the east side of the stream. It was owned and worked by Ian McMahon, a second-generation Irishman. Ian was one of the first to arrive in the basin from New York City. When rumor of gold first came out of the black hills, a boot maker by trade, the call of riches from the Dakotas and the potential for a better life encouraged him to sell his business and try his luck digging for gold.

He didn't know much about mining, but on the way to the Dakotas he crossed paths with another Irishman who lived in Buffalo Gap. This was before Langston had turned it into a bustling mining town. Due to their common ancestry the two hit it off. With Sean's experience in mining coupled with Ian's financial support, the two formed a partnership that brought them to the basin and the opening of the McMahon mine. Progress had been slow at first but with the arrival of the Buffalo Mining Company and their help Ian and Sean were able to get enough gold from their claim to keep them going. Now, within the past two weeks their fortune seemed to be improving. More gold was being drawn from the shaft with indications it could produce large amounts.

Brian and Sarah caught a glimpse of Ian going into the entrance as the two approached the sluice. Stopping next to the wooden canal that allowed the water to separate the gold from the rest of the soil, Brian said to Sarah, "We'll wait here for him to come out."

Sarah said nothing in response but stopped next to Brian and placed her hand to her forehead just above her eyebrows to block the sun. She leaned forward peering toward the opening in the mine to obtain a better view. Her wait wasn't long. Within moments Ian came from the entrance carrying a wooden crate. The man sported an athletic build with strong arms and shoulders. The red hair upon his head was matted down and in need of a good washing. An equally bushy beard of the same color covered his square jaw. The shirt he wore was made of cotton, buttoned down the front, and it too needed a good cleaning. The pants were the best-looking item in his ensemble. Being new, they had not yet succumbed to the dirty work of mining. As he carried the crate from the mine Brian and Sarah could tell from his struggle that it was heavy.

Just then Ian caught sight of Brian and Sarah and grunted in a slight Irish accent, "Morning to ya." He then waddled to the right of the mine's entrance and bending over dropped the heavy load onto the ground next to the sluice. Rising back up, the Irish miner slapped his hands together and turned to the two watching him and blurted with a big smile, "Welcome! I'm always glad to see you Mr. Dolan!"

"It's good to see you Mr. McMahon. How are you today?"

"Couldn't be better," boomed the Irishman, "the sun is shining and the fact that the mine is showing some kindness never hurts."

"Glad to hear it," said Brian, looking to the sky to acknowledge Ian's reference to the sun's rays.

"And, Miss Schuler, you are sure a pleasant sight for sore eyes," remarked Ian with the wink of his eye.

"Thank you Mr. McMahon," replied Sarah with a slight smile, "you are too kind."

With a roaring laugh the miner exclaimed, "Now I've never been associated with being overly kind. Give me time Miss Schuler and we'll see if you feel the same. Anyway, come around the sluice and we'll let you take a look inside the mine."

Brian and Sarah worked their way around the sluice to the where Ian was waiting to shepherd them into the mine. As they entered Brian scrutinized the walls and ceiling of the mine noticing it was constructed similar to the other mines he had been in. The ceiling was close to six feet high allowing plenty of headroom for Ian and his two guests. The walls and ceiling were held in place by logs cut from the available forest along the edge of the basin. These were placed at regular intervals of approximately five feet. Reaching the first support Ian snatched a kerosene lantern from the nail lodged in the log on his right. From his front right pocket he pulled out a match that he struck on the base of the lantern and lit the wick. As he adjusted the flame the light it threw permitted the three to see as far as two supports ahead of them.

The miner looking at the two next to him warned, "Be careful. The footing can be uneven and at places the ceiling juts down so you may have to bend over when passing through. If you see me duck, do the same."

"Thanks for the warning," said Brian then extending his hand down the tunnel, "we're in your hands."

With a slight nod of his head, Ian unhurriedly moved his way down the tunnel. Within the first ten steps or so Brian and Sarah became aware of the temperature change from the mine and the outside. The coolness of being underground was quite apparent and refreshing, though for Sarah, the musty smell that came with it was a bit bothersome. After another twenty steps, they reached the first of the protrusions. There was no way of continuing without crouching. Ian stopped just before the outcrop and pointing at it and said, "Watch your head."

He bent down and scooted beneath the rock for several feet then stood up again. The two behind him did the same. When all three were standing erect, Ian nodded his head toward the outcrop, "That rock is a real nuisance. Especially when dragging a load of dirt to the entrance. Having to crouch while hauling a heavy load gets old pretty fast."

"I bet, since your prospects have improved recently, you have been willing to put up with that inconvenience a little better," offered Brian.

"True enough---"

"Isn't that a light up ahead!" interrupted Sarah.

The two men snapped their heads in the direction Sarah had indicated. She was correct. They both could make out a low glow of light.

"Is that Sean?" asked Brian

"Can't be," answered Ian with a puzzled tone, "Sean went off to Buffalo Gap last night. He won't be back to well after noon."

"Anyone else have a reason to be in your mine?" inquired Brian

"Not that I know of," replied Ian with furrowed brow.

After a moment, the surprise in Ian's eyes had turned to curiosity and he said, "Let's find out who it is and why they're in my mine."

With that he cautiously headed down the tunnel with his lantern stretched out in front of him. The three moved steadily along the tunnel with eyes focused on the light ahead, each wanting to discover who was creating the glow. As the light from Ian's lantern came closer to the glow ahead the tunnel became much brighter. But, even with the extra light, the three were unable to see who was creating the light ahead of them. The tunnel took a sharp jog to the right just before the light. As they neared the corner, their steps slowed and they inched their way to the edge of the turn. Peering around the corner they saw a lantern on the floor of the tunnel and next to the lantern was an indistinguishable bundle. There was no one in sight.

Ian was the first to move to the lantern on the floor of the tunnel, closely followed by Brian and Sarah. Standing over the lantern the three immediately recognized the bundle that lay a couple of feet from them partially buried in the base of the tunnel wall. Dynamite! A roll of five held together with twine. The three looked at each other perplexed and Ian said what all were thinking, "What is a bundle of dynamite doing here?"

From behind them a voice spoke that startled the three-standing next to the dynamite, "To cave in the mine of course."

Turning to face the voice their eyes met a small scrawny man that was balding and wore clothes that looked to be a size too big. The man was pointing a pistol at them and the smile on his face was not friendly. Due to a small indentation in the wall of the tunnel the man had been able to squeeze up against the wall without being noticed.

"What do you mean, to cave in the mine?" demanded Ian.

"I going to put you out of business," shot back the scrawny man.

"But why!" exploded Ian.

"I believe I can answer that," interrupted Brian. "The pattern is becoming clear. When a mine begins to be somewhat productive, as yours has, an accident of some sort occurs making the digging of the gold no longer possible."

Shaking the pistol at Brian the scrawny man sneered, "aren't you a clever one." Spitting tobacco juice out the side of his mouth he continued, "No matter. In a very short time none of you will be able to tell what you have come to figure out."

"What do you mean?" asked Brian.

"Can't leave any witnesses to reveal the truth about another accident within the mines," answered the scrawny man with the unfriendly smile returning to his lips.

"Why you!" shouted Ian as he lunged at the scrawny man with outstretched arms.

Before he traversed two steps there was a crack from the pistol and Ian collapsed to the floor of the tunnel. The scrawny man was not as stupid as his appearance would suggest. He quickly fixed his eyes on Brian. Pointing his six-gun, he commanded, "Don't get any ideas and keep your hand away from your gun!"

Brian had begun to reach for his pistol but slowly raised both hands above his chest upon seeing the muzzle end of the scrawny man's pistol pointed at his chest.

"So I won't have any further trouble, lady, would you slowly take the gun from Mr. Dolan's holster."

Sarah carefully reached with her left hand and gripped the butt of the pistol.

"That's it," encouraged the scrawny man, "Take it by the handle only, and carefully pull it out."

Sarah did so, and when she had it completely out, she was instructed to toss it toward the entrance of the mine. She did so without hesitation and the pistol landed with a thud some 30 feet up the tunnel. Just then they heard a moan from Ian. He was on his back lying motionless, the look on his face revealed the pain the wound was causing.

"He needs help, "insisted Sarah.

Before the man with the pistol could answer another painful moan came from Ian.

"Okay," said the scrawny man annoyed, "If it will keep him quiet. Just no funny business and Mr. Dolan you stay where you are."

"Give me your scarf please," said Sarah to Brian holding out her hand.

Brian reached into his back pocket, pulled out the scarf and handed it to Sarah. She then knelt next to Ian and saw where the bullet hand entered the miner's body. There was a bloodstain the size of a double eagle gold coin on the dirty cotton shirt just below Ian's shoulder. Unbuttoning the first three buttons of the wounded man's shirt and lifting gently the portion with the stain from the wound Sarah saw that there was a small hole were the bullet had entered the shoulder. There was still a slight oozing of blood coming from the wound. Taking Brian's scarf she placed it directly on the wound and applied as much pressure as the pain would allow.

"He's going to need medical attention," stated Brian looking from Ian to the man pointing the pistol."

"Actually, he isn't," said the scrawny man keeping his eyes trained on Brian. "I 'd shoot him now, but I don't want to take the chance of the shots being heard. I doubt anyone heard the first one."

"What's your plan then?" asked Brian.

"To blow this mine up with you in it," responded the man waving his pistol gesturing he meant all three. "Everyone will think it is just another unfortunate accident and conveniently all witnesses will be buried with the evidence."

"That's murder!" exclaimed Sarah.

"When it comes to gold some have no qualms about murder," stated Brian.

"So true and I aim to get my share of it," snarled the scrawny man. "So if you would be so kind as to move yourselves down the tunnel away from the dynamite," demanded the man gesturing with the gun.

"What about Ian?" asked Brian.

"Take him with you. I don't want to run the chance of any of you interfering with the dynamite or fuse," he barked.

While Brian and Sarah helped Ian to his feet, their antagonist backed up against the tunnel wall while keeping a vigilant eye upon his prisoners. Crouching to the floor of the tunnel, he picked up a burlap bag that had been sitting against the wall. Rising slowly, he motioned for the three to move farther into the mine. After forty feet, he commanded them to stop and lowered himself slowly placing the burlap bag on the ground. He fumbled through it and drew out of it a spool of twine. Throwing it at the feet of the three he said," Ma'am I would like you to take that twine and tie the hands and feet of these two men."

Sarah and Brian carefully sat Ian against the tunnel wall and Sarah retrieved the twine. It took about ten minutes to complete the job. When Sarah had finished, both men sat upright with their hands behind their backs against the wall. It was evident that Ian was having difficulty with the position his body was in, the pain clearly showing on his face. Then it was Sarah's turn. The scrawny man had Sarah un roll the proper amount of twine, and then cutting it with his knife, he tied her hands behind her back. Sitting her next to Brian and Ian he tied her feet together. Stepping back he looked at the three sitting against the wall with great satisfaction on his face.

"That should do the trick nicely," said their captor as he turned and picked up the burlap sack, "the dynamite will either bury you or you will be trapped inside to suffocate to death."

In a raised voice Brian said, "I don't believe you're doing this on your own. Out of curiosity, who's your boss?"

The scrawny man didn't say anything at first. He just stood there mulling over what Brian had asked. Finally he said, "I suppose it won't do no harm to tell you. That information will soon be trapped with you forever in this mine. Besides it will be amusing to see your reaction when you find out."

Chuckling to himself, he walked back and forth in front of the three captives. On his fourth pass he stopped suddenly and turned to face them. With a sneer slowly growing on his mouth he asked," Any guesses?"

The three sat silent.

"No guesses huh? No matter, I'm sure you would have been wrong anyway."

Cocking and uncocking his pistol nonchalantly he said, "I take my orders from the main man in Buffalo Gap."

The scrawny man could see the brains of the three working to take in the information he had just given them. Then he saw all three come to the same conclusion.

"Not true!" cried Sarah.

"I assure you it is true," asserted the man standing before them.

"Why would Mr. Langston be involved in something such as this?" enquired Brian. "He has a mine of his own that is producing well, besides that, as head of the only mining company in the territory he controls most of what comes out of the other mines as well."

"Not going to tell ya," retorted the little man. "Because I don't know. I just follow orders and get paid well for doing so. Which reminds me, time to finish this job"

Spinning to his left he headed back up the tunnel grabbing the lantern the three captives had brought into the mine. The three couldn't see what the man was doing because of the bend in the tunnel, but they could hear him finishing the preparations for setting off the dynamite.

Brian looked toward Ian and saw he was working on the twine that tied his hands together. It didn't look as though he was making much progress. Looking to his left he saw Sarah with her eyes closed, chin slumped on her chest.

"Are you all right Sarah?" he said quietly.

She remained silent and he was just about to ask her again when she lifted her head and opened her eyes and said, "Oh, I'm okay. I was just praying."

"Praying?"

"Yes, praying. I was asking God for his guidance and praising him that I was not alone at a time like this.'

"Not alone? You mean that you are here with Ian and me?

"Yes and also that God is with me and I can trust Him in all things."

"You can trust that He will get us out of this predicament?"

"If that is his will. But because He gave me salvation I know what ever happens it is for my good and His glory."

"To be buried alive?" stammered Brian.

"If it is---"

"I hate to interrupt," cut in Ian, "but we don't have much time before the dynamite explodes. Shouldn't we spend the little time we have getting as far away as possible?"

Brian and Sarah looked at each other, then toward Ian.

"Quite right," agreed Brian, if you think it will do any good."

"If we get far enough away at least we stand a chance not being buried by the rock and dirt," said Ian in between gasps.

"Can you move?" queried Sarah.

"Yes. If we move fast, there is a short off shoot perpendicular to the main tunnel just a few feet from us. If we can get inside it, we will be somewhat protected from the blast," answered Ian as he lowered his upper body to the floor of the tunnel and began rolling further down the passageway. His two companions followed his lead and rolled along the floor in the same direction. It was difficult to find their way in the dim light but Sarah and Brian found out quickly that Ian was correct; there was a smaller shaft that cut off at a forty-five-degree angle from the main tunnel. Ian had already rolled into the tunnel when Brian and Sarah reached the entrance to the smaller shaft. With some maneuvering the two were able to work themselves into the shaft next to Ian. The three of them lay on the floor their eyes squeezed shut and their muscles tensed in anticipation of the exploding dynamite. After several seconds of silence, Brian opened his eyes slowly and looked in the direction of the other two. Then it happened. The tunnel was filled with a tremendous roar as the dynamite exploded.

Chapter 12

Brian lay on the floor of the small tunnel the three of them had rolled into just before the dynamite detonated. His eyes were closed due to the dust still settling from the explosion. After a minute he slowly opened his eyes and saw only darkness. Rotating his head he hoped to get a glimpse of some ray of light but it was to no avail. Complete, total darkness. The explosion had done the job their nemesis had intended. The force of the explosion had collapsed the walls and the ceiling completely filling the tunnel with rock and dirt.

Brian's attention was directed to his left when he heard either Sarah or Ian moving.

"Is everyone alright?" said Brian into the darkness.

For a short moment there was no answer then a muffled voice said, "I'm alright."

It was Sarah. Brian recognized her voice but it seemed far off even though he knew she should be right next to him. Then he heard another voice, it too was muffled like Sarah's, " That was a close one, if not for this side tunnel we would have been goners for sure."

Brian then realized the voices were muffled because his eardrums had been affect by the loud blast. He hoped it was only temporary.

"Ian how are you doing?" Brian asked directly.

"As far as the explosion, I'm still alive. As far as the gunshot, I'm still alive," said the miner in return. Rolling on his side to face the direction of Brian's voice he added, "Seriously, under the circumstances I'm doing just fine."

"Glad to hear it," said Brian, then as an afterthought he added, "Speaking of hearing, the explosion seems to have affected mine. I am having difficulty hearing you two."

"Mine seems to be fine," said Sarah

"I don't notice any difference," stated Ian.

"Okay, I guess it's just me. You might want to speak up until this passes," offered Brian.

"What now?" asked Sarah with concern.

" I doubt we can dig ourselves out from this side," uttered Brian, "the blast brought down too much dirt and rock and we have no tools.

"I disagree," challenged Ian, "we can dig our way out and without much trouble to boot."

No one could see the expressions on Brian and Sarah's faces because of the total darkness but if a light had been available the shock on their faces would have been quite clear.

"Your crazy Ian!" burst Brian. "How can we dig through all that rock and dirt with our bare hands? Not only is the tunnel full of debris, but I'm pretty sure there are large chunks of rocks we couldn't even begin to move,"

"You are correct Mr. Dolan," replied Ian calmly, "if as you say, we attempt to dig out the main tunnel. But it just so happens we have another way to go."

"Another way?" prompted Sarah.

"Fortunately for us we had this side tunnel to protect us from the blast of the dynamite but it is also our way out of this mine," said Ian.

"How so?" asked Sarah.

"You see, when we were first digging the main tunnel it led us down this side shaft, but after a bit, the gold petered out and we broke through to the outside. The shaft was not producing so we blocked the opening with timber and dirt. Unless a person was right next to it, no one could tell there had been an opening. It shouldn't take much effort to move the timbers and dig our way out," explained Ian with a grin on his face that neither Sarah nor Brian could see.

"Well Ian, I am sorry the side tunnel didn't produce, but in the end, I'm mighty happy we now have this potential escape route," said Brian with relief, then, directing his voice toward Sarah he added, "Sarah you keep praying, it seems your prayer earlier has been answered."

"Continue to pray I will, but you can pray yourself anytime," replied Sarah out of the darkness.

"Pray! Me!" cried Brian, "But I'm not a Christian."

"Anyone can pray to God," encouraged Sarah, "

"How do I do that?" asked Brian puzzled.

"First, by asking for forgiveness of your sins," returned Sarah.

"I don't know, my past is pretty corrupt," said Brian somewhat discouraged.

"Christ died for all sins," urged Sarah, "Tell the Lord you are sorry and ask Him to help you follow Him. He will forgive you."

"Hey! I'm as religious as the next man," declared Ian, "but can you two have this spiritual discussion at a later time? We need to be thinking about getting out of here."

There was silence in the dark for a moment then Brian spoke, "Quite right Ian. First we need to free ourselves from these bindings then we can tackle the dirt and timber at the end of this shaft."

The three shuffled on the floor of the shaft as they attempted to loosen the twine that bound their wrists. At first there was little success. It was hardest for Ian. Each time he twisted his wrists a shooting pain wracked his shoulder from the gunshot wound. Struggling with the twine Brian realized it would take forever, if at all, for him to free himself. Lying on his back he relaxed and contemplated the situation. Then it came to him.

Scooting on his back along the tunnel he searched the floor with his fingers. After a minute he found what he was looking for. Pushing his body up against the wall Brian was able to position his wrist against a rock the size of a small cannonball. The importance of the rock was twofold. First, it was anchored in the floor of the shaft and second it had a jagged edge. It was the perfect device to cut through the binding holding his wrists together.

After two minutes of rubbing his wrists back and forth he was able to cut through the twine enough that he could pull his wrists free. He then quickly removed the cord that bound his feet. In short order he had the other two free from their bindings.

"How far to the end of this shaft?" inquired Brian in the direction he surmised Ian to be standing.

"Not far at all. Twenty yards at the most, "stated Ian

"I'll lead us down the shaft. Both of you place your hands on the wall and we'll slowly work our way to the end," directed Brian as he put a hand on both Sarah and Ian guiding them to the shaft's wall.

Taking their time the three gradually made their way along the wall of the tunnel. Even though they took small steps each one of them stumbled several times as they moved toward the end of the shaft. The complete darkness and a rough surface made finding footing a challenge. No one said a word, the only sound coming from the scraping of their boots over the floor of the shaft. After several minutes Brian's voice jumped out of the darkness, "I believe we've reached the end of the tunnel."

"Good," said Ian, "let's get to digging."

"I believe Sarah and I will do the digging," said Brian with concern.

"I agree," concurred Sarah, "we can do what needs to be done."

"Well, if you insist. I'm not liken it, but I do feel a bit woozy," admitted Ian

"Sarah work your way around Ian and come along side me and we'll start on this area just to my right. The dirt seems looser here," charged Brian.

Sarah did as Brian asked feeling her way around Ian and ending up on Brian's right with her hands on the dirt in front of her. The dirt was loose compared to the wall of the shaft they had just navigated. Sarah was able to dig her fingers into the soft dirt and pull large clumps of cool soil away from the wall. Brian and Sarah worked without speaking, their full concentration was on removing as much earth as quickly as they could. Even with only their hands to work with they made good progress. After a couple of minutes Brian partially unearthed one of the timbers that sealed up the opening to the outside.

"Ah now we're getting somewhere," said Brian when he realized what he had before him, "Sarah I've reached one of the timbers. Let me clear the dirt so I can feel what can be done."

"Of course Brian," responded Sarah stepping gently back from the portion of the wall she had been working on.

Brian then cleared the soil away from the timber that was about waist high. Working upward and downward from where he had first touched the timber he guessed the timber to be about eight inches in diameter. He also discovered there were other timbers above and below the one he had uncovered. Brian then scrapped off as much soil from the timber as he could. Once he had most of the soil removed from around the timber he moved to the far left of the tunnel and pushed with steady pressure on the log. The log moved faintly.

"Excellent!" cried Brian with excitement.

"What is it?" demanded Sarah.

"The timber moved when I pushed on it. That means we'll be able to remove them without too much effort." answered Brian, "We're that much closer to being out of here."

"What can I do to help," asked Sarah with relief in her voice.

"Hold on just a second. I have a question for Ian first," replied Brian.

"What is it," came Ian's voice from the darkness.

"Do you remember how many logs you piled up when sealing this opening?"

"Let me see," said Ian pausing for a moment then continuing, "I think five, maybe six."

"Ok. Then there should be no more than two logs at the most above the one I have cleared the dirt from," stated Brian. Then to Sarah he said, “Sarah feel for the log I have cleared and we'll work on freeing the two above it so we can pull them out first and work our way down. Does that make sense?"

"Yes." replied Sarah as she groped for the log Brian had indicated.

The two of them then worked diligently on removing the earth from the logs situated above the one that had been exposed. When the dirt had been removed from the two upper logs Brian directed Sarah to the far right and instructed her to pull on the upper most timber on his signal.

"Ready?' asked Brian.

"Ready!" barked Sarah while grasping the top timber with both hands.

"On three. One. Two. Three!"

On three the two pulled and the log broke from the dirt more easily then the two had expected. It literally jumped from the wall and both Brian and Sarah leaped backwards allowing the log to crash to the floor in front of them. The log bounced straight up about a foot where it hit the floor then rolled back toward the wall. The shaft slanted downward to the blocked opening more sharply than any of them had realized.

Brian and Sarah were able to remove the next two logs without much difficulty. As soon as they had the three logs pulled from the wall Brian and Sarah excavated the dirt in front of them. It was not hard packed which made digging with their hands possible. This went on for about five minutes when suddenly from where Brian was digging a sudden burst of light exploded into the dark shaft. They had reached the outside.

"Oh, Thank you Lord!" breathed Sarah.

Even with the sun's rays coming in through a hole the size of a child's head, the brightness where it had been completely dark moments before caused all three to shut their eyes instantly. They took several moments to adjust to the sudden availability of light.

"Told you there was another way out," said Ian joyfully.

No one responded. Brian stepped to the hole and peered through it. Nothing met his eyes but the sparse pines that became thicker as they worked their way up the ridge. Making sure there was no one outside Brian withdrew his head from the hole and began digging around the edges of the opening. It wasn't long before he had cleared enough of the dirt and rock that would allow each of them to crawl through it to the other side.

Turning to Sarah he said," Sarah you first. Then you can help Ian as he comes through."

Sarah moved to the opening and crawled through. Reaching the outside, Sarah rolled to the ground over her right shoulder and ended up on her side directly below the opening. Wasting no time she got to her feet and positioned herself in front of the opening waiting for Ian to come through.

Just as she had, Ian came through the opening with outstretched hands. Sarah crouched her body below Ian's hands and guided them onto her shoulders while she clasped her hands around his forearms. As Brian pushed from behind, Sarah took as much weight as she could upon her shoulders, while at the same time guiding Ian carefully down the slope to the ground. Once completely outside Sarah steered Ian to the left helping him into a sitting position with his back against the outside wall.

Brian immediately followed crawling through the hole and coming down the outside similar to the way Sarah had, rolling over his right shoulder. Once at the bottom he popped up quickly and immediately brushed the excess dust and dirt from his shirt and pants. Sarah shadowed Brian's action by brushing as much of the loose soil from her clothing. When satisfied with the results she looked at Brian and asked, "What are we going to do now?"

Brian didn't respond immediately, he was looking toward Ian. After several seconds he brought his attention to Sarah and said, "Now that we have escaped from being buried in the mine I'm thinking we can use this disaster to our advantage."

"Oh really," responded Sarah crossing her arms onto her chest, "This I want to hear."

"As I see it, no one knows we survived the blast and if they presumed we did they will think we are still stuck inside the mine. With the size of the explosion my guess is that it will take quite a while for them to get through all the rock and dirt that is blocking the tunnel. Also we know that Sean is in Buffalo Gap and won't be here to suggest going around the section of cave where the explosion occurred by using this side shaft we just came out."

Brian paused and scrutinized Sarah's face looking for confirmation she understood where he was heading with his explanation. He didn't have to study long, for she said, "Keep going. I think I see where you're headed with this."

"Good. So, I 'm sure we can be pretty safe to assume that everyone will presume that we didn't survive the cave in. That's what we can use to our advantage. If everyone thinks we are dead we are free to investigate behind the scenes without interference."

"What's our next move?" interrupted Ian.

Walking over to Ian, Brian said, "First thing is to get you to a doctor," Kneeling next to the wounded man, Brian lifted Ian's shirt collar and examined the bullet wound.

"You are fortunate it was only a 36 caliber he used. They don't make as large a hole as say, a 45 colt."

"It feels big enough," groaned Ian.

"The bleeding has stopped," stated Brian placing the collar gently back over the wound, "but we need to get that bullet out of there as soon as possible."

"There's no doctor in the camp," related Ian, "we tend to take care of each other when the need arises."

"Then we'll have to get you to Buffalo Gap as quick as possible," said Brian. "And this will help us with the other thing that needs to be done.

"Which is?" ask Sarah when Brian didn't offer to say what the second item was.

"We need to follow up on what our man with the dynamite said in the mine about your uncle. Is he really behind all that has been going on with the mines and if so, why?"

"I hope it isn't so?" said Sarah with furrowed brow.

Chapter 13

At the entrance of the McMahon mine a crowd of men had gathered. Most everyone in the camp had rushed to the mine's entrance immediately after the explosion. There were several men already inside the mine attempting to clear the debris from the collapsed portion of the tunnel. Those that remained just outside the entrance had their full attention to the work going on inside the mine.

This made it easy for Brian, Sarah and Ian to maneuver towards the upper end of the sluice behind the large water trough. They had worked their way along the depression that ran along the main tunnel and parallel to the entrance of the mine. Then, with all the interest being focused on the rescue, the three were able to scurry to their present location.

Whispering as he kept an eye on the mine entrance Brian said, "We need to get to our horses so we can get Ian to Buffalo Gap and a doctor. Once that is done then I can go see Langston and confront him about what the guy in the mine said."

"Do you think Ian is well enough to travel that far?" inquired Sarah with a soft voice.

"We don't have choice," replied Brian continuing to keep his eyes on those at the mine's entrance, "Buffalo Gap is the closest place that he can get the proper care so we'll have to do our best to keep him comfortable while traveling."

"I'll be alright, Sarah" assured Ian. Turning to Brian he said, "Let's get a move on."

"First we'll get your horse," directed Brian patting Ian on the shoulder, “then we'll work our way back to the main office and pick up the other horses."

"My horse is just behind us near that clump of pines," stated Ian pointing over Sarah's shoulder.

"Right---"said Brian then suddenly became silent.

"What's the matter?" asked Sarah.

"Oh, I just wish I still had my six gun," responded Brian a little irritated, “I'm thinking it might come in handy in the near future."

"Your welcome to mine," interjected Ian, "It'll be more useful in your hand than it would be in mine, the way I'm stoved up."

"I accept your offer," replied Brian, "Where is it?"

"It's in my tent underneath my pillow," explained Ian, "the cot on the left as you enter the tent." As an afterthought he added, "Oh and there's a box of cartridges under the cot."

"Sarah you take Ian with you, collect his horse, and I'll meet you both in front of the office after I retrieve the pistol," instructed Brian.

Sarah took Ian by the arm and leading him in the direction of the clump of pines the Irishman had pointed out. Brian watched them for several seconds then turned toward Ian's tent and in a crouch silently made his way to the front of the canvas structure. Without hesitating he pulled back the flap and ducked inside. Brian could tell instantly this was a place habited by men. There were two cots one on each side of the tent. Each cot had a pillow and a couple of blankets. The blankets were disheveled and strewn haphazardly over the cots revealing the tent hadn't been tidied for quite some time. Wasting no more time in studying the interior of the tent, Brian scooted to the cot on his left and lifted the feather filled pillow at the head of the cot.

Lying on the cot, as Ian had said, lay a pristine 1873 model colt pistol. Taking it in his hand Brian thought with a grin on his lips, "he may not care for his living quarters but he surely takes pride in his firearms. I can't fault him for that"

Half cocking the hammer he spun the cylinder and saw that the pistol was fully loaded. He let the hammer back down and placed the colt into his holster. Not a perfect fit but close enough it would cause no problems while carrying it or if he needed to, draw it quickly. Brian then looked underneath the cot and saw a nice looking black derby sitting on top of a well-worn overcoat. Brian was again surprised at this discovery. He didn't realize that a person that mined for gold in the wilds of the South Dakota Territory would have a care about their possessions let alone their appearance. Evidently with the pistol and this sharp looking hat Ian cared for both.

Gently lifting the overcoat so not to disturb the black derby on top Brian searched for the box of cartridges underneath. With the first sweep of his hand he contacted the box and withdrew it from under the overcoat. On the box in bold letters was written "Winchester Metallic Cartridges 45 Caliber". Shaking the box slightly Brian determined the box was nearly full. With gun in holster and extra cartridges in his hand Brian returned to the entrance of the tent, stretched out his hand and opened the flap just enough to view the outside.

Brian had an unobstructed view of the mine and all the men gathered in front of the entrance. Every one's attention was still focused on the rescue attempt within the mine. Glancing swiftly to his left and then to his right, Brian saw no one else in view. He was about to slip through the flaps of the tent and make his way to the office when he heard voices off to his right. Scrunching into the corner of the tent as far as he could without touching the tent itself he listened to the conversation just outside the entrance.

"I really don't know," said a man with a squeaky voice.

"Can you believe it!" barked a second voice much deeper, "Another mine caved in."

A third voice joined in, "I've heard of bad luck, but this is getting out of hand. It's getting to the point it's almost not worth the effort."

"This time it's supposed to have involved the new foreman Dolan and the lady that came here with him, Langston's niece. Jacobson said he saw the two enter the mine with Ian then after several minutes there was the explosion," said the deep voice man.

"Is that the skinny guy with one of the first mines on the other side of the stream as you come up the basin?" inquired the man with the squeaky voice

"That's him," verified the man with the deep voice.

"Ya, Jacobson said he didn't see anyone leave the tunnel before the explosion occurred," said the third voice.

"Are you saying they didn't make it out," asked the man with the squeaky voice.

"Not me, that's what Jacobson said," declared the third voice.

"Mr. Langston's not going to like that," said the squeaky voice.

There was a pause in the conversation then Brian heard the voices again but they were further away. Brian surmised they had moved toward the mine. Waiting for a couple minutes, Brian listened for any other voices or movement. There were none, so Brian slipped through the entrance of the tent and made his way silently and with as much speed as possible toward the office where the other two would be waiting for him. He darted through the scattered pines keeping the large ones between him and the men gathered at the mine.

As he made his way to the office building he thought of the statement the scrawny man had presented back in the mine. Was Langston involved in all that had happened in connection with the mines the past couple of months? And if so what role did Langston have for Brian in this scenario?

Chapter 14

As the main office building came into view, Brian saw Sarah and Ian in front of the steps leading up to the door. Actually Ian was adjacent to the steps propped on his left side on the front edge of the porch with his left hand covering the bullet wound in his shoulder. The two were furtively scanning the area in front of them when they spotted Brian coming out of the pines. Sarah gave a short wave as Brian approached her and Ian. Brian's attention was completely on Sarah, even in this situation, after just surviving a mine cave in, her wholesome beauty stood out and Brian found he didn't want to avert his eyes from Sarah's face as he scampered toward them. He realized then that his interest in this young woman was more than just an acquaintance between two people thrust together through circumstance.

But his attention was diverted when Ian moaned faintly. Looking in Ian's direction Brian saw that the wound in his shoulder was giving the man some discomfort but there seemed to be no bleeding.

"How are you doing?" asked Brian calmly.

"I'll make it. Don't you concern yourself with me," answered Ian with a grimace on his face as he stepped from the porch to the horse in front of him, "Just you help me up on this flea-bitten animal and let's get a move on."

The Irishman grabbed the saddle horn with his left hand and placed the toe of his left boot into the stirrup hanging along the side of the horse. Brian quickly moved to his side and taking hold of his right leg lifted the wounded man up into the saddle. The move brought another groan from Ian's as he wrapped his leg up over the saddle. Taking a deep breath Ian said trying to be convincing, "See, nothing to it."

"We'll see," returned Brian with some doubt in his voice. "We have a bit of a ride ahead of us." Turning to Sarah he nodded his head toward her horse and said, "Up you go." Sarah took the reins of her horse, and gripping the saddle horn, flung herself onto the back of the horse. Brian followed suit and after settling himself into the saddle he said, "We'll work our way along the east ridge of the basin keeping in amongst the pines. That should give us plenty of cover to bypass all those down at Ian's mine."

The Buffalo Mining Company foreman tapped the side of his mount with his heels and pulled on the reins directing the horse into the pine trees. Ian fell in behind Brian and Sarah. Brian worked his way up the basin picking his way through the trees so as to make as little noise as possible. As the troop progressed, the trees became more numerous. Even so, Brian was able to maneuver easily amongst the pines. The undergrowth was sparse allowing the horses to travel through the trees comfortably.

Shortly the three were even with Ian's mine and as they made their way along the edge of the basin they could see the miners bunched together outside the mine entrance. All of the men's attention were fixed on the entrance and what was going on inside the mine. It appeared to the three that those at the mine were still attempting to clear the shaft and hadn't discovered the three of them were no longer in the mine. This suited Brian just fine. The longer it took the miners to discover they had escaped the blast, the more time Brian had to investigate Langston and his involvement in the recent accidents within the mining camp.

Once the three had traveled some distance pass the mine, Brian led the group back down to the river's edge and followed the trail he and Sarah had trekked when coming to the mines earlier. By now they had bypassed all of the working claims, and there was no chance of discovery by anyone within the basin. Brian kept their pace slow as they worked their way down the trail. He would have preferred a faster speed, but after checking Ian's condition several times, he realized the wounded man's injury wouldn't allow it.

It took a couple of hours for the trio to reach the area where the ambush of the gold shipment had occurred. As they came to the trail there was no evidence left to indicate a small battle had transpired recently. Brian led Ian and Sarah to the rocks they had hid behind during the ambush and charged them to take a break. It was early in the afternoon with a cloudless sky, but even though it was June, the heat of the summer had not yet arrived, so the need for shade was minimal.

Brian and Sarah dismounted and moved to Ian's horse where they both carefully helped the wounded man down from his horse. They then gently escorted him to the nearest boulder and lowered him against it. Ian laid his back against the warm rock closed his eyes and let his upper body relax. After a moment and without opening his eyes Ian said, "What is your plan Brian, from this point on?"

Before answering Brian took a spot next to Ian and placed his back against the boulder and let his frame slide slowly down the face of the rock. Once seated, he tilted his face toward the sun, soaking in the warmth from the sun's rays and allowing his muscles to relax.

"First thing on the agenda is to enjoy this short time of rest," said Brian closing his eyes as he laid his head back against the boulder. "Then once we reach town, we get you to a doctor."

Coming up next to the two sitting on the ground Sarah turned her back to the boulder they were sitting against and let her body fall gently against the warm surface. Joining the conversation she asked Ian, "How you holding up Ian?'

With his eyes still closed Ian responded, " The pain's not as bad as it was when we were in the mine, though I'll be mighty happy to get to the doc."

Opening his eyes and swiveling his head toward Brian he asked calmly, "Can the doctor be trusted?"

"I think so," answered Brian without hesitation, "The short time I was around him I came to believe he was an honest man doing his job the best he knew how."

Looking at Brian, Ian said with a grin, "Glad to hear it. I don't know if I could come to grips with having you take this bullet out if we couldn't depend on the doc in town. No offense."

"Certainly, no offense taken. I'm just as glad not to have to do it," agreed Brian.

"What do you plan on doing next? That is, once we have Ian taken care of," interjected Sarah.

"Well," said Brian thoughtfully, " I believe the next item of business is to visit your uncle and see if he can't shed some light on all that has been going on in Buffalo Gap and the mining camp."

"Do you think he's involved?" asked Sarah with apprehension, "I mean in a way that's not good?"

"I hope not," returned Brian without much confidence in his voice, "A lot could be explained though if he is and with my experience with him back in New York, I wouldn't be surprised."

"People can change," said Sarah emphatically, "God can change the heart of the worst sinner."

"I can't speak to God's involvement in this but I do agree that people can change," concurred Brian with sympathy in his eyes, "I know I'm not the same person I was when I worked with Langston back in New York and I had hoped that he had changed as well. It was one of the reason I decided to come to Buffalo Gap in the first place."

"Langston or not, we need to find out who is behind all the mayhem at the mines. Good men have been killed, which has convinced others to quit," snarled Ian.

"Well, maybe we'll get some answers when I visit with Langston," said Brian.

After Brian's statement the three-kept quiet for several minutes pondering their own thoughts while letting the warmth of the sun soak into their tired muscles. The rest was greatly welcomed by the three, but after a short while, Brian slowly got to his feet and turned to Ian, grasped him under his left arm and shoulder and gently raised him from the boulder. Sarah followed suit and grabbed Ian's other arm and shoulder and the two were able to get the wounded man to his feet with only one slight groan from the Irishman. Brian and Sarah guided Ian to his horse and carefully helped him into the saddle. The two then got onto their own horses and with the kick of his heels on the flanks of his horse, Brian headed south, leading the other two in the general direction of Buffalo Gap.

It took two hours to reach Buffalo Gap after leaving the boulders. They saw no one along the way and the terrain was flat and mostly rolling hills of grass. As they approached the town and before it came into view Brian took the little troop off the main road and worked his way east toward some abandoned out buildings he had noticed the previous time he had been in Buffalo Gap. To look at them one would guess they had been constructed before the discovery of gold in the hills to the north. They were weathered and the smallest of the three structures had a roof that sagged in the middle. This suited Brian just fine, his plan was to leave the horses at the buildings and take Ian to the doctor on foot, out of sight of the main street. He was in no hurry to have the townspeople or Langston, know the three were in town. They had to deliver Ian to the doctor first.

Once at the buildings, the three immediately dismounted and Brian and Sarah took the three horses into the largest building tethering them to a ladder that led to a loft at the back. The three then moved to the opening to the barn and carefully surveyed the ground between themselves and the town. Brian figured it to be about fifty yards. At the moment there was no one in view and after a couple of minutes of watching, it looked as though it would remain so.

If Brian's memory served him the doctor's office was just three buildings down from where they stood. There was nothing between the out buildings and the town itself. If they were to be discovered, it would be as they made their way across this open area. Waiting for it to get dark was not an option, it was too far off and they needed to get Ian to the doctor soon. Brian decided they would just have to take their chances. Even if discovered, it wasn't certain they would be recognized.

"Can you make it to the doc's office without our help?" inquired Brian placing his hand gently on Ian's uninjured shoulder.

"Just lead the way," shot back Ian with a grin.

" Okay, just walk normal as though we belong here and are just heading back to town," instructed Brian stepping out of the barn.

Ian put on his best poker face and walked briskly by Brian's side, matching his pace as they headed across the open area toward the buildings that lined Main Street. Sarah stepped lively to Brian's other side and the three walked together. No one saw them traverse the fifty or so yards and once across, they stopped. There was no movement or sound, so Brian slowly looked around the corner of the building into the narrow alley.

There wasn't a soul within the alley though Brian did see several people pass along Main Street at the other end. After several moments, no one else showed themselves. Brian waved for Ian and Sarah to follow him to the next alley. In a short time they had made their way to the doctor's office. Brian held up his hand to signal for the two behind him to stop. Again he waited and listened. No sound so he once again carefully gazed around the corner and eyed the alley.

The alley was similar to the one they had just passed except Brian noticed a door half way down the alley leading to the doctor's office. Turning to the two behind him Brian said, "There's an entrance from the alley into the doc's office. I'm going to go see if it is unlocked. If it is you can follow me in. If not, I'll return and we can decide if we want to enter through the front doorway."

Both Ian and Sarah answered with the nod of their heads. Brian slipped around the corner and made his way to the side door. Sarah moved up to the corner and warily looked into the alley to watch Brian. Upon reaching the door Brian took a quick glance look toward the Main Street. Nothing stirred. Bringing his attention back to the door he cautiously pushed it open a couple of inches.

Brian stood silently holding the doorknob listening. He took another swift glanced toward the Main Street, seeing nothing, he gently pushed the door ajar. When there was enough space for him to squeeze through the opening into the room he stopped and listened again for any sound or movement from within the structure. Still there was no sound. Brian then poked his head into the room. At first it was too dark to recognize anything but after several seconds Brian's eyes began to adjust to the light coming through the open doorway and he was able to distinguish objects in the room.

The room was not large, maybe seven feet by twelve feet. Along the walls were rows of shelves filled with various types of wooden boxes, jars and canisters.

Stepping back into the alley Brian motioned for Sarah and Ian to join him. They did so without drawing attention and the three ducked through the doorway. Brian left the door ajar just enough so they would have enough light to maneuver within the room. At first no one said anything while the three allowed their eyes to adjust to the dimness of the room. Then Sarah spoke with a hushed voice," Looks to be a storeroom."

"My thoughts exactly," agreed Brian and then added "A welcome bonus."

"What do you mean by a welcome bonus?" asked Ian

Just then the doorknob on the interior door began to turn.

Chapter 15

Before the knob had finished its turn, Brian pushed the outside door closed just enough that no light entered the room but not all the way so as to make a noise. At the same time he drew his pistol from the holster on his right hip and held it ready at his waist. Sarah and Ian rushed to the interior wall and flatten themselves with their backs up against the shelves. By then the doorknob finished its turning and the door opened into the room. There was a sudden burst of light that flooded into the room from the doorway.

The man coming through the doorway didn't notice the three in the room at first. His attention was focused on his vest pocket where his hand was fumbling for something within. After a moment he drew out a match and looked into the room. Right away he noticed Brian standing in the light coming through the door from behind him. The man with the match froze with a startled look on his face.

"Take it easy," said Brian with a hushed voice, "don't move and don't make sound."

The man in the doorway remained still and just stared into the eyes of Brian.

"Okay, come into the room, slowly, and close the door," directed Brian as he stepped backward to the door that led into the alley. Not taking his eyes off the man with the match he opened the outside door just a crack while the man with the match closed the inner door.

"You can go ahead and light the lantern," charged Brian.

The man moved somewhat shakily to a small table sitting against the wall. Reaching for the lantern the man lifted the glass and struck the match he was holding on the edge of the table. The match flared and the man holding it lighted the wick and lowered the glass chimney onto the base. He then turned the flame up so the room was fully lighted. That's when the man standing next to the table discovered there were two more in the room with Brian.

"Take what you want. I'll not stop you. But be aware that this room contains medical supplies and if taken you will put others health at risk." said the man that just lighted the lamp.

"Don't worry," chuckled Brian putting his pistol back in his holster, "were not here to rob you Doc." Pointing to Ian, Brian continued, "This man here has been shot and we brought him here to utilize your services."

With a puzzled look the doctor asked," Why didn't you come through the front door?"

" I guess this looks a bit strange," agreed Brian with a slight grin, "Circumstances forced us to avoid the front entrance, in short we didn't want to be seen as of yet."

The doctor had a medium frame that was a bit on the thin side. He had on a long sleeve white cotton shirt with the arms rolled loosely up to his elbows. Over the shirt he wore a brown vest that was slightly too big, as were the blue pants that completed the ensemble. He looked to be in his mid-forties with a touch of gray in his hair just above his short sideburns.

The doctor relaxed and said while moving over to Ian who was leaning with his back against the shelf on the wall, "I'll get your explanation about not coming through the front door later. Right now, I believe I need to take a look at this man's wound."

"Thanks, Doc. That would be much appreciated, "winced Ian as he pushed himself from the shelf he was leaning on.

Lifting Ian's collar, then the make shift bandage over the wound, the doctor made a swift but thorough examination of the damaged area. Once satisfied, the doctor lowered the bandage back over the wound.

"You're a lucky young man, in several ways," stated the doctor.

"Oh really!" said Ian with doubt in his voice. "How do you figure?"

Clearing his the throat the doctor answered, "First off, it looks to be a small caliber bullet, anything larger would have tore you up with a much larger hole. Second, it looks as though you haven't lost too much blood. That's very important. And finally who ever took care of your wound and this bandage did an excellent job of keeping the area as clean as possible. Again, very important. So with these three things your chances of surviving are good to excellent."

"Okay, I stand corrected," said Ian sheepishly.

"But we must get that bullet out right away." said the doctor sternly. Clutching Ian's arm the doctor carefully pulled the wounded man toward the inner door. "Let's get you into the other room and we'll work on getting that piece of lead out of your shoulder."

Guiding the young Irishmen to the door the doctor yanked it open with just enough force to swing the door against the adjoining wall with a tap. Gesturing for Sarah to go ahead of him, Brian followed, closing the door behind him. The doctor had brought them into a room twice as large as the storage room they had just left. Right away Brian recognized they were in the room where the doctor did his work. Brian was immediately impressed. For a small town located far from any large city the office was furnished with what looked to be the latest equipment and instruments. To his left was an immaculate table for patients to be worked on. This is where the doctor escorted Ian and then asked him to sit on the table. Once Ian was on the table, the doctor opened a cabinet directly behind Ian and with a quick search of the middle shelf, procured a pair of scissors.

"Is this a good time to ask what your story is?" inquired the doctor as he grasped the bottom of Ian's shirt upon returning from the cabinet. As the doctor began to cut the shirt Ian looked toward Brian with an expression on his face that conveyed the unspoken question, "What do you think? Should we tell the doctor the truth?"

"Well doc, a couple of years ago I would have spun a tale so far from the truth a map wouldn't help you find your way. But these days, I find the truth is usually the way to go. Especially from the few things I have heard about you, I get the sense that doing right is more important to you than doing what's easy." After a moment's pause Brian continued. "While at the mining camp this morning, we stumbled upon a man in the process of blowing up Ian's mine. Ian was shot and we were left in the mine to be buried by the explosion. Long story short, we were able to survive the blast and dig our way out through an abandoned shaft. Wanting those that planned the mine explosion to believe we didn't survive we snuck away from the mine and worked our way back to town to get Ian to you for help."

Cutting up through the shirt and through the neck line the doctor responded to Brian's telling of the story with a deep sigh then said with disgust to no one in particular, "When is this going to stop? When I first came here just over a year ago it was a peaceful quite town. Now it seems we have some kind of trouble every other day."

"I know what you mean," concurred Brian, "When I first came to Buffalo Gap I wasn't in town but a few hours when there was a shooting in the saloon. Once Sarah and I arrived at the mining camp, trouble showed itself there too."

"And we can add the ambush of the gold shipment to Fort Meade to that list," said Sarah.

"What can be done?" requested Ian as the doctor gently removed the dirty bloodstained shirt from Ian's body.

"Hard to say," responded the doctor while throwing the dirty shirt into an iron bucket next to the table. "It's come to the point I don't know who to trust."

"Well," interjected Brian, "The first thing I can do is visit Langston and have a talk with him about the trouble at the mine and see if that can shed any light on what's been going on."

"Can he be trusted?" asked the doctor as he gestured for Ian to lie down.

"I don't know, the man that shot Ian said that Langston was the one behind all the trouble but maybe he said it to divert our suspicion from the real person in charge. I hope to find out for sure when I speak with Langston," replied Brian.

" It is still hard for me to believe that someone, whoever it is, would go to such extremes to hurt and kill people for selfish gain," exclaimed Sarah.

"Greed is a mighty powerful sin," said the doctor.

"I've seen what it can do to the meekest of men. If the promise of quick riches is placed before them some will pursue that wealth no matter who or what gets in the way." said Brian moving to the end of the table where Ian's head lay.

Looking to the doctor he asked, "What do you think Doc, will it take much to get the bullet out?"

"No, it looks pretty straight forward. The only problem, since it looks to be somewhat deep, is, it will be painful unless you let me put you under with ether." answered the doctor turning his eyes to meet Ian's.

"Doctor, I'm not much into pain, so go ahead with the ether," encouraged Ian.

"Good," nodded Brian, "then I'm going to head on over to the Buffalo Mining Co. office and see if Langston is there."

"I'm coming with you!" said Sarah, more forcibly than she had intended.

Before Brian could respond the doctor spoke, "Actually--- Miss, I could use your help with the extraction of the bullet, that is, if you'd be willing?"

Moving to the cabinet again the doctor withdrew a bottle of ether and placed it on the stand that was at the foot of the table Ian was lying on.

Speaking to Sarah again the doctor continued, "It makes it much easier if I have someone handling the ether while I extract the bullet."

Sarah pondered the doctor's request for a moment in silence then said, "Alright, if it will help I would be glad to assist."

The doctor responded with a smile, then went to the washbasin against the far wall and washed his hands and gathered a few instruments to perform the procedure.

"If you are set then I'll head over to see Langston," said Brian.

"Yes go, "affirmed the doctor waving his hand toward the door.

Stepping over to Sarah, Brian held her hand with his two. Looking into her eyes he said, "Thanks for all you done, including staying here to help Ian. Keep up hope; we don't know what your uncle's involvement is in all this. Maybe you could pray for him while I'm on my way over there. In fact you could say a little prayer for me also," with a smile Brian turned to the door behind him and headed to the front entrance of the building.

After closing the door leading to the street, Brian paused on the wooden sidewalk and took a deep breath to gather his thoughts. He wasn't quite sure what he would discover in his conversation with Langston. Sure, Langston had been implicated as the one in charge of all the trouble but that was only by word of mouth and only from one source. He would be guarded in their talk with Langston yet he would allow Langston the benefit of the doubt and approach the conversation with an open mind.

Gazing down the street toward the middle of town Brian saw several people on the sidewalks and in the street. He didn't recognize any of them and no one looked as if they cared who he was. Adjusting his gun belt, Brian made sure it and the holster were hung comfortably around his waist and hip. He then walked steadily across the street his eyes taking in all that was around him as he approached the office of the Buffalo Gap Mining Co.

Upon arriving at the office door, all remained quiet. Without hesitating, Brian stepped onto the sidewalk, instantly opened the door and entered the office.

As Brian came through the door he saw Langston sitting behind his large table scrutinizing some papers in his hands. On the table in front of him were other papers randomly spread out. As soon as Brian passed through the doorway Langston raised his head. At first there was just a blank look on his face but this quickly changed to a look of surprise. Laying the papers in his hands onto the table he blurted, "Brian!"

"Good evening, Virgil" said Brian with composure.

"Why are you here?" shot Langston, then calming himself he continued, "There must be some kind of trouble, to bring you back to town."

Ignoring the question Brian said, "Trouble? Yes, I would definitely agree there is trouble."

Langston looked intently at Brian waiting for him to continue but Brian stood in silence looking at the man behind the table with a furrowed brow.

Langston said with a growing grin on his lips, "Tell me what the trouble is? I am sure whatever it is, it's not as bad as your face shows."

"To begin with, I am sure you heard that the gold shipment we were riding with was ambushed a couple hours out of town," responded Brian

"Yes, yes," said Langston impatiently, " I was informed of that incident the day it happened. Fortunately, it failed and the gold was able to reach Fort Meade. Of course, it isn't surprising for such a thing to occur with the temptation of so much gold in one spot."

"Were you informed that a couple of soldiers were killed during the ambush?" asked Brian.

"Yes I was. Unfortunate, quite unfortunate, "answered Langston with sympathy in his voice.

"What about the mines?" inquired Brian crossing his arms over his chest, "You didn't fill me in on the troubles they were having before you sent me up there. As foreman, it would have been nice to be aware of the situation before arriving."

"Yah, sorry it had to be that way. The truth is, I left you out of the loop on purpose. I didn't want you to be biased when you took over. I wanted you to run things as you saw fit from your own perspective. I remember how you did things back in New York, and I believed that's what is needed here."

Brian unfolded his arms and said, "If you remember our first meeting the day I arrived in Buffalo Gap, I let you know then that I may not be the same guy you worked with back in New York."

"Did you?" responded Langston leaning on the edge of the table with thumbs on top and fingers curled underneath. "Can't say I remember that specifically, but even so, if a man does change, there's always a little bit of what he was before that remains. That's what I'm counting on with you."

"I think you are going to be disappointed, "stated Brian.

"Oh I don't think so. Not after you hear what's at stake," encouraged Langston.

Just then the front door to the office opened. Brian immediately turned to his left and looked toward the door. Right away he saw the silver star on the vest of the man moving into the room.

"Sheriff Baker! Come on in," barked Langston moving around the table and gesturing toward Brian, "Look who's here."

The sheriff quietly shut the door then faced Brian and nodding his head said, "Mr. Dolan," then turning to Langston he said," I thought I recognized him from down the street just as he stepped onto the sidewalk in front of your office. I came down to your office to confirm it was him and to see why he was here in town."

"Trouble at the mining camp has brought him back to town," said Langston.

"Oh is that all?" said Sheriff Baker with a grin.

" I would give the situation at the mines more than, is that all," interjected Brian.

"Would you?" responded the sheriff, the smile disappearing from his lips, "What is your impression then Mr. Dolan, specifically?

" The fact that men are dying and---"

"Now Brian," cut in Langston, "mining is a hazardous under taking and there are bound to be some accidents and some of those accidents will unfortunately result in deaths."

"I don't disagree with you Virgil, to a point, "replied Brian turning his attention back to Langston, "but the nature of the accidents and when they are occurring, along with the ambush, it appears there is more at hand then just coincidence."

"What are you suggesting?" inquired sheriff Baker suspiciously.

"I believe there is one or more people directing these incidents," answered Brian while watching for the two men's reaction to his statement.

The sheriff looked toward Langston. The owner of the Buffalo Gap Mining Co. shook his head slightly. Brian could tell from this slight communication that his statement had had an impact on the two men. Then Langston spoke, "Do you have an idea who this person or persons might be, "probed Langston.

"Not exactly," said Brian, "I was hoping you could help with that."

Langston didn't respond right away. He slowly moved back around the table and sat down picking up one of the papers he had been looking at when Brian first came into the office. Studying the paper for a moment he finally looked up at Brian and said with a stern look on his face, "You're correct in your assumption about the accidents. They are not just a coincidence. The truth is, as I believe you have already suspected, this company is behind all the trouble that has occurred the past few months." Langston paused for just a moment then spoke the next words slowly and deliberately, "The question now is, what are you going to do about it?"

Chapter 16

Brian took what Langston had just said and mulled it over. He stood still, purposely not reacting to the words he had just heard. He had not expected Langston to be so forthcoming as to admit being behind the trouble at the mines. He wondered what Langston's ploy was and why he revealed it so easily. He didn't have to wait long for an answer.

"From your reaction, or should I say, lack of one, I can't tell how you feel about what I just told you," said Langston, leaning forward and placing his elbows on the table and his hands together, "Let me explain, and I am confident you will understand my position."

Before continuing Langston glanced toward Luke and nodded his head directing the sheriff to back away from Brian. Luke promptly obeyed and moved a few feet away from Brian. Drawing his gaze back to Brian, Langston said, "After New York I was pretty down and out. I drifted here to there until I came across Mrs. Bailey in Springfield, Illinois. She was a widow of two years, and we hit it off right away. She wasn't rich, but her previous husband left her comfortable with property and a home when he died of tuberculosis. We were married within two months of our first meeting and after a month of marriage I heard of the discovery of gold in the Black Hills of Dakota. I didn't think much of it at the time but then my wife had an unexpected accident going to town from our ranch in the country. She was found at the bottom of a ravine next to the wagon and horse she was driving. The only explanation given was the horse must have spooked and while running along the road the wagon veered too far to the edge and went over taking Mildred and the horse down with it."

Langston paused took a breath then continued, "I was devastated, of course, and couldn't remain in Springfield. Thinking of the gold in the Black Hills, I sold all that I owned, and came out here to try my luck at mining. Before going into the Black Hills, I saw the potential Buffalo Gap presented to be the doorway to the mining district and its gold. I took the money from Mildred's property and began investing in Buffalo Gap. At first I just concentrated on providing the tools the miners would need to mine for the gold up in the hills. This brought in a quick return that allowed me the capital to begin investing in the growth of Buffalo Gap and to bring it to what it is today."

Langston paused again and Brian took the opportunity to interject, "If things have gone so well, why did you begin causing all the trouble the last several months?"

"Good question," admitted Langston, "Just like before in New York, the town grew faster than I could keep up with financially. My vision got ahead of my assets. The wise thing would have been to slow down and let things catch up, but like an addicted gambler the power and money drove me on. Soon, I had much more money going out than coming in and bills piled up. Plus investors from back east I had brought on board wanted their investments to begin to pay off. They weren't, so I had to resort to other methods to make it all work."

Langston leaned back in his chair dropped his hands onto his lap and continued, "I didn't have the time to stake my own claims and hope I would strike it big, so, I adapted by taking over those that had already been producing well or had signs of beginning to do well. Out here, where the law is scarce, it wasn't difficult to create the impression that the accidents at the mines were just that, accidents."

Suddenly the opening of the front door interrupted the conversation. All three men diverted their attention to the front of the office. As the door opened into the room, the three men recognized Langston's niece, Sarah.

"The plot thickens," said Langston standing up from his chair, "Sarah please, do come in, and if you wouldn't mind, close the door behind you."

Sarah followed his directive and closed the door then walked over to where Brian stood.

"I should have guessed you wouldn't leave Sarah at the mining camp by herself, how unfortunate," said Langston shaking his head. Then speaking to the sheriff he said, "Luke would you pull the blind and lock the door so we won't have any more unwanted interruptions."

Moving quickly to the front of the room Luke did as Langston asked, first pulling down the blind over the one window to the outside, then throwing the bolt to the door. Once done, he moved back to where he had stood when Sarah first came into the room.

Brian spoke first, "What do you mean by, how unfortunate, when referring to Sarah being here?" asked Brian.

"I had intended not to have Sarah and her family know of all that we have spoken of. They were to be innocent of all my dealings here in Buffalo Gap and in the Black Hills. I owed her and her family that much after all that had happened in the past," answered Langston.

"What is he talking about?" demanded Sarah with eyes on Brian.

"The short of it is, your uncle is the one behind all the troubles here in town and the mines," said Brian with contempt.

Before Sarah could respond Langston said to Sarah, "I am truly sorry you have become involved to this extent. As I said, my intentions were to have you unaware and innocent."

"And live a lie!" cried Sarah, "I'm glad I found out the truth."

"With that said, I am now forced to give you both two choices. But first Brian, think back to New York. We almost had it made there, working together. I didn't know how to overcome our troubles then, but here I have the wealth we dreamed of back then and it's at our fingertips to be taken and used. That's why I brought you here; together, I know we can control this town and this area for years to come. The choice is yours, to join our operation and become a productive part of it, or decline and be eliminated."

"Eliminated? You couldn't, you wouldn't, "said Sarah aghast.

"Sarah, face the facts," consoled Brian, "your uncle has stumbled onto a gold mine so to speak. He has changed some since I last worked for him. He is facing similar problems here as he did in New York but this time he has learned to adapt and turn a disaster into a productive enterprise. He is not going to give that up if at all possible. If that means he has to kill to do so, he feels it is worth the risk." With a grin Brian spoke directly to Langston, "At first I didn't see clearly the genius behind his scheme, but now I understand the beauty of it. With the reputation he has built up in the town and along with having the law on his side the chances of anyone discovering his true intentions are pretty slim. Even if someone suspects and begins to investigate or complain, your uncle uses the law to take care of the agitator. No one is the wiser. How can I, no, how can we," said Brian turning to face Sarah, "refuse such an opportunity." He then gave Sarah a slight wink. With Langston to Brian's back and the sheriff behind Sarah, the only one to catch the wink was Sarah, herself.

Looking back at Langston, Brian said, "You are correct Virgil, your proposal is to inviting, we're in."

Eyeing Sarah, Langston inquired suspiciously, "Are you sure, that both of you are fully with the plan?"

Hearing the doubt in her uncle's voice Sarah responded forcefully, more than she had intended, "Uncle, my family has lived a simple life all our lives, here is an opportunity to change that, and besides I have learned to trust Brian's instincts this past week so if he says it's an opportunity waiting, I won't pass it up."

"Good to hear," remarked sheriff Baker moving next to the big table, "it would have been such a waste if you have made the other choice," then speaking to Langston he asked, "can we really trust these two?"

"Oh, I think so," said Langston, "Brian wasn't the best right hand man back in New York because of his good looks. No, there was an inner ruthlessness that drove him to get the job done no matter what. It was just a matter of the right incentive to rekindle that drive."

"Now that we are a part of the organization and before I go back to the mining camp wouldn't it be wise for Sarah and I to know who are on your payroll," suggested Brian.

Langston didn't answer right away. Instead he leaned forward, placed his elbows onto the table, clasped his hands together, and rested his chin upon his hands. He squinted his eyes and looked slowly back and forth from Brian to Sarah. After a moment he said slowly, "What do you think Luke?"

Luke followed Langston's lead and took a short time to consider the question the man behind the table had just put forth. He was quicker to give his answer than Langston had been.

"They're going to need to know sooner or later. May as well let them know now."

"I agree," approved Langston turning his attention to Brian and Sarah, "Obviously Luke, here, is with us. The others from town include Charles Whitmore, the owner of the mercantile, Trevor Callahan, who runs the stables at the other end of town, and Buck Hagan, the saloon owner. Of course there are others that are not prominent members of the community that we hire to do the undesirable tasks that come about."

"What about the mining camp? Anyone there?" asked Brian.

"We have one, his name is Frank Willard and he's in charge of encouraging the miners to give up on their mines. He's proven to be pretty good at his job," replied Langston with pleasure in his tone.

Sarah took a quick glance at Brian and Brian met her glance with a look of his own. He conveyed with his eyes that he recognized, as she did, that Frank was the scrawny man that attempted to kill them in Ian's mine.

"I'm sure I'll get to know each in time, especially Frank, since I'll be spending most of my time at the mines," stated Brian nonchalantly then turning his gaze upon Langston he asked, "What now?"

"It's getting on near dinner time and I'm famished. I say, let's have supper and we can hash out the details over that." recommended Langston.

"I didn't realize I was hungry until now, great idea," said Brian patting his stomach lightly, "we haven't eaten since this morning,"

"I could use a bite of food," said Sarah softly.

"Before we go though, I need to take care these documents," stated Langston pushing the papers on the table together then picking them up and tapping them on the tabletop as if he was gathering cards together after a hand of poker, " Luke will you go find Jim and have him come to my office so he can file these documents correctly?"

"Yes sir, Mr. Langston, I'll be right back," replied Luke shortly.

It took him four quick steps to reach the door and the same number of seconds to unlock it, open it, and disappear out into the street. As the door shut behind Luke, Brian moved up to the table. He tried getting a look at the papers Langston was organizing, but the owner of the Buffalo Mining Co. was too fast, and they were all neatly stacked together. Langston then placed them at the far end of the table, too far for Brian to get a look even at the top sheet.

"Do you keep all your records in this building? " inquired Brian.

"Everything is filed in the back room," replied Langston.

With Langston's answer barely out of his mouth, Brian strode to the front door, locked it, then lifted the blind a couple of inches and peered through the window. Langston and his niece followed his actions in bewilderment. After a moment Brian lowered the blind and then made his way across the room to the door that led to the back room. He opened the door and surveyed the room on the inside.

"Can I help you with something?" uttered Langston.

Brian ignored his question and scrutinized the room a few seconds more, then gently shut the door. Moving back next to Sarah he turned and faced Langston.

"Langston, I told you earlier that I may not be the same person you knew when we worked together in New York. After that fiasco, during the next year and a half, through self-examination and through new friendships I realized what we had done was not right. And I pledge to take a new direction for my life. As a culmination of that new direction I am now an agent for the Department of Defense. Mr. Langston, you are under arrest for robbery, extortion, misrepresentation, attempted murder and murder."

Langston stood in silence staring at Brian with a blank expression. Sarah's expression on the other hand, showed her total surprise of the revelation just brought forth by the man she had met a week ago. Stepping back a couple of steps she scrutinized the man standing before her, trying to absorb the information she had just received. Brian kept his eyes focused on Langston. The man behind the table kept his face blank. Slowly his lips curled into an evil smile.

"Quite sneaky, I must admit. I would have thought this was a joke but I can tell from the look on your face that you are rather serious. But," then pausing for a moment before continuing, "you have no proof and it is only your word against mine."

"I have your confession of guilt and a witness in Sarah here to back me up." replied Brian gesturing to Sarah.

"Hah!" retorted Langston. "How do you know she's on your side? The promise of money and a life of luxury are most tempting."

"Brian has my full support," charged Sarah, "money has never been a priority in my life, I trust in the Lord to supply my needs."

"It's still my word against yours," reminded Langston pointing to himself then to both Brian and Sarah, "and remember I control this town."

"I bet not the whole town," expressed Brian, "there are some here you don't have in your back pocket. Besides I am sure I have all the proof I need in that back room of yours. My guess is you have a paper trail that will lock you up for years."

The evil smirk on Langston's face disappeared in a flash. The full realization that the records in the filing cabinets in the back room could connect him too much of what had been going on the past year hit him like a ton of bricks. He took a furtive look to the door leading to the back room then swung his head toward the front door. Reaching calmly into the pocket inside his jacket Langston said with composure, "You might have something there, but, it won't do you any good if you can't get to it," From inside his jacket Langston pulled out a derringer which he cocked and pointed at Brian.

"I don't think you'll use that, " stated Brian.

"And why not?" asked Langston with raised eyebrows.

"How are you going to explain shooting me with Sarah as a witness?"

"That's easy. I shoot her also," answered Langston nonchalantly.

Again there was silence. Langston could tell by the look on their faces that the last statement had baffled them both. He thought, *they truly don't understand whom they were dealing with.*

Then Brian spoke, "You're not thinking straight."

"Yah, how so?" sniped Langston.

"If you shoot us both, how are you going to explain what happened?" inquired Brian while slowly lowering his hand next to his holster then stated, "When sheriff Baker left we were all in agreement and on the same side."

It was Brian's turn to see his question had caused some doubt to enter Langston's mind. But within an instant, the evil smirk returned to the man's lips.

"You forget, as I did for just a second, the only explaining needed to be done is letting Luke and Jim know you two had a change of heart and your presence was a danger to the company. We've already done, as you know, what needs to be implemented to protect our interest. So, there is no worry about explaining. We'll sweep you two under the rug, so to speak, and business goes on as usual."

"Your telling me you can shoot Sarah---" began Brian turning his head slightly toward Sarah. As he did, Brian kept Langston in view out of the corner of his eye. Just as he had hoped Langston averted his gaze toward Sarah. Instantly Brian dove to his right, while grasping the handle to the revolver in his holster and drawing the weapon as he fell to the floor. Startled, Langston took a hurried aim at Brian and pulled the trigger. The sound of the tiny pistol exploded throughout the room. The bullet from the derringer zipped over Brian's left shoulder and slammed into the wall.

Brian quickly rose to one knee and had Ian's six shooter at eye level aimed at Langston. The owner of the Buffalo Mining Co. frantically brought the barrel of his derringer in line with the man kneeling on the floor before him but Brian's gun barked twice before Langston could pull the trigger. At this distance both bullets easily found their mark, the first driving deep into the chest just below the throat and the second splintering the left collarbone. Langston crumpled to the floor as if he was a puppet that had just had its strings cut.

No one moved. Brian remained on one knee pistol ready, while Sarah stared at the limp body of her uncle on the floor behind the table. Once Brian was sure Langston wasn't a threat, he holstered his pistol and moved over to the table and knelt next to Langston. At Brian's movement Sarah made her way to the other side of her uncle. As she knelt down she kept her eyes on her uncle's face. His eyes were open and he was still alive but Sarah could tell he was having difficulty breathing.

"Is there anything you can do for him?" asked Sarah looking at Brian.

Brian answered with a slow shake of his head. From the location of the blood-soaked stain on Langston shirt he could tell the bullet had destroyed the lower trachea. Langston was having trouble breathing and it wouldn't be long before he literally suffocated to death. Sarah softly grasped Langston's left hand and closing her eyes and bowing her head began praying quietly. Brian watched Langston's niece for a moment and was suddenly touched by the tenderness she was displaying toward a man who had just said he would shoot her to protect his own interest. In response, he closed his eyes and bowed his head.

Just as Sarah finished with her prayer a large gurgle came from Langston's throat and his eyes closed followed by the relaxing of his body. He was gone. Brian took a quick glance at Sarah, then jumped to his feet and picked up Langston's derringer off the table. Holding it out to Sarah, who was now standing, he said, "Here, take this, it only has one shot left but one shot is better than no shot. When the sheriff returns who knows what will happen."

Sarah took the pistol and Brian could tell right away she was accustomed to handling firearms. The first thing she did was break the barrels open and check the two cartridges. Satisfied she lowered the barrels back into place. Noticing Brian eyeing her she said, "My father made sure, I could take care of myself, riding a horse and handling firearms were two of the first lessons he taught me." Sarah then slipped the pistol into the right pocket of her pants and asked, "What do we do now?"

"Good question," responded Brian as he looked first toward Sarah's uncle, then to the front door, "I not sure if anyone heard the shots, though my guess is that they probably were. So that means we will have company shortly."

Going to the window Brian peeked out through the edge of the blind. Observing no movement in the street or along the sidewalk he turned to Sarah and instructed, "I want you to go back to the doctor and fill him in on what happened. Then you two get the deputy and bring him back here. I believe his name is Jasper."

"Can he be trusted?" cut in Sarah suspiciously.

"I believe so," said Brian with confidence, "thinking back, before going to the mining camp, I got the impression he wasn't part of Langston's dealings. We're going to need his help. My position with the Department of Defense will only go so far way out here in the middle of nowhere, especially when the sheriff is one of the bad guys."

"What if he doesn't believe our story?" questioned Sarah with a deep furrow in her brow.

"I trust the doctor will convince the deputy. Anyway just bringing him here will make him aware of the situation. Have him gather as many of those in town he trusts and bring them along."

Scooping up the papers on the table he continued, "I'm going to check the files in the back room and obtain as much evidence as I can so we'll have the proof necessary to reveal what the Buffalo Mining Company has been doing."

"I'll be back a soon as I can," stated Sarah moving to the front door. After unlocking the door she turned her head back in the direction of Brian and gave him a look that told him to be careful. Then she left the office closing the door behind her.

Chapter 17

Once she left, Brian took the papers from Langston's table and went into the back room. It was small, no windows or doors that led to the outside. The back wall consisted of three large file cabinets. The wall to his left was bare while the wall to the right had a small table with two whisky bottles, one full the other three quarters full and three drinking glasses. The only other item on the table was a kerosene lantern that Brian immediately lighted to give more light to the darkened room. A quick perusal of the top cabinet drawer convinced him he had enough information to prove Langston and the Buffalo Mining Company conducted illegal operations.

Just then the sound of the front door opening came to Brian's ears. Blowing out the lantern the man from the Department of Defense laid it on top of the file cabinet then made his way quietly to the doorway to the office making sure he kept from view.

"Whoa, what's going on here?" exploded a high-pitched voice from within the office, "is that Mr. Langston on the floor?"

Hugging the doorframe with his right side to keep from being seen Brian heard two men scuffle across the office floor.

Then the high-pitched voice spoke, "He's dead. He's been shot."

Peering around the door jamb Brian saw sheriff Baker and Langston's assistant, Jim kneeling next to Langston's motionless body. The sheriff had his six-gun drawn. Brian pulled his own pistol from its holster and stepped into the main room and commanded, "don't move!"

The two men across the room snapped their heads in the direction of Brian. Sheriff Baker instinctively raised his pistol.

"Don't think about it!" said Brian firmly, "If you would put your pistol on the table, slowly, it would be much appreciated."

Sheriff Baker stared at the pistol in Brian's hand. After a moment, he made his decision and laid his pistol gently on the table.

"Good choice," acknowledged Brian with the nod of his head, "if you both would raise your hands---"

"What's the meaning of this Mr. Dolan?" interrupted the sheriff with a snort and anger in his eyes.

"I'll explain as soon as you two have moved away from the table," answered Brian with a steady voice. Jim responded first moving slowly to his right. The sheriff followed suit carefully making his way along the back of the table. Suddenly the front door was pushed open. Brian took a quick glance at the doorway. Before he could distinguish who was coming through, Sheriff Baker lunged for his pistol on the table. Brian caught the sheriff's movement out of the corner of his eye and sharply swung his attention back onto the two men near the table. By then Sheriff Baker had the pistol in his hand and was bringing the barrel in line with Brian. Brian was faster. With a slight adjustment he aimed roughly and squeezed the trigger. The bullet crashed into the sheriff's right forearm causing him to drop the pistol. It hit the side of the table before rattling onto the floor. The sheriff gave a muffled grunt as he grabbed his arm and pulled it next to his body.

From the doorway came the rasping voice of the deputy, "Hold on everyone! No one move." Looking to the doorway Brian saw several people, some already inside, while most were still outside. The first to meet his glance was the deputy with six-gun drawn and at the ready in front of his right hip. There was a look of determination upon his face. Just behind his right shoulder was Doc McMillan with a double barrel shot gun held across his chest. Behind the doctor was Sarah followed by other people Brian didn't recognize.

"I'm glad you are here deputy," quipped Brian, "your assistance is greatly needed."

Moving into the middle of the room the deputy scrutinized the scene before him. First looking toward Sheriff Baker and Jim he asked not so politely, "How's the arm?"

"It hurts!" growled Sheriff Baker, then nodding toward Brian, "arrest Dolan he's gone crazy. First he killed Langston then he shot me when I confronted him with it."

Deputy Cunningham crouched down and looked under the table

where the dead body of Langston lay.

"That's not the version told to me by the young lady." Said Cunningham calmly as he stood up. "Her version puts Langston taking the first shot after he confided his illegal doings to the young lady and found out Mr. Dolan is an agent from the Department of Defense."

The color faded from the sheriff's face upon hearing the news of Brian's affiliation.

"It was all Langston's and Baker's doing!" cried Jim with a look of horror on his face. They made all the plans and gave the orders---"

"Shut your mouth!" snarled Baker as he lunged at the quivering man. Baker slammed into Jim and the two fell against the wall. Even without the use of his right arm the sheriff got his left hand on the throat of Jim and pushed him hard against the wall. Instantly, Deputy Cunningham and Brian dashed forward and together pulled the sheriff off the man he was choking.

Gasping for breath, Jim spat at Baker, "I'm not going to hang for your dirty work!" Then looking directly at the deputy and Brian he added, "I took care of the paper work and ran their errands, that's it."

Sheriff Baker seethed with anger but there was little he could do while in the grasp of Cunningham and Brian.

"It would seem the old adage of "you can't determine a book by its cover" is quite appropriate when it comes to several prominent men of Buffalo Gap," said the deputy thoughtfully. "It would seem the same goes for you as well Mr. Dolan."

"Yes, sorry I had to remain undercover, but until I was sure who was a part of the problem, well---" said Brian raising his shoulders sheepishly.

"We'll talk later but for now we need to get these two locked up and take care of Langston's body," said the deputy.

The deputy proceeded to direct two men from the doorway to take charge of Langston's body and get it over to the doctor's office. Meanwhile, Sarah came into the office and made her way next to Brian, but before either could speak Deputy Cunningham spoke," I would like to speak with you both at the sheriff's office after I get these two settled. Say, in about thirty minutes. There is much we need to clear up."

"I agree, there is much we need to discuss," concurred Brian.

Sarah and Brian watched the deputy and his two prisoners disappear through the door. Turning they faced each other. Sarah broke the silence, "I'm glad that you're safe."

Brian didn't answer right away. Looking at her lovely face he was struck by the depth of feeling in her eyes and the warmth of her expression. Taking a step closer he gently reached out for her right hand and took it into his own. Then Brian said with a smile, "I'm sure that your prayers helped.

Sarah dropped her eyes, the look on her face showed that she felt Brian's statement was mocking her religious convictions. Brian, recognizing the look, lifted her eyes to his by softly taking her by the chin and raising her head.

"Sarah, I truly meant what I said. Over the past week, I have come to appreciate your faith. So much so, that I would like to learn more from you, once all the logistics of this Buffalo Mining Company situation is put to rest, we need to speak seriously.""

A shy smile came to Sarah's face.

"In fact," continued Brian, "I would very much like to discuss several things with you when this is all done."

" I'll look forward to that, "returned Sarah her smile becoming more confident.

"Until then, we have to wrap up this Buffalo Mining Company fiasco. Decisions must be made about what to do with the mining company, and how to replace Sheriff Baker," stated Brian.

Locking her arm with Brian's, Sarah said as she guided him to the door, "Sounds like we'll be busy for a while, so, we better get started."

Made in the USA
Columbia, SC
17 September 2017